The World Is But a Broken Heart

# THE WORLD IS BUT A BROKEN HEART

## MICHAEL MAITLAND

*Signature*
EDITIONS

Cover design by Doowah Design.
Cover photograph by Lode Van de Velde, Creative Commons Public Domain.
Photo of Michael Maitland by Alan Worsfold.

This book was printed on Ancient Forest Friendly paper.
Printed and bound in Canada by Hignell Book Printing Inc.

Many thanks to Diana Jones, Ada Robinson, Judith Berman, Elizabeth von Aderkas, Gillian Bridge, Debra Henry, Greg Stone, John Barton and Karen Haughian.


We acknowledge the support of the Canada Council for the Arts and the Manitoba Arts Council for our publishing program.


**Library and Archives Canada Cataloguing in Publication**

Title: The world is but a broken heart / Michael Maitland.
Names: Maitland, Michael, 1957- author.
Identifiers: Canadiana (print) 20230466397 |
Canadiana (ebook) 20230466400 |
ISBN 9781773241296  (softcover) |
ISBN 9781773241302 (EPUB)
Subjects: LCGFT: Short stories.
Classification: LCC PS8626.A4179 W67 2023 | DDC
C813/.6—dc23


Signature Editions
P.O. Box 206, RPO Corydon, Winnipeg, Manitoba, R3M 3S7
www.signature-editions.com

*for*
*Katherine*
*Jessica*
*&*
*Abigael*

# CONTENTS

# NEW YEAR'S EVE

Except for the dull whir of the stove clock, the house is silent. The kitchen light bleaches Maureen's skin, making her look older than she is. Her worn slippers scrape over the linoleum as she walks to the back door. The cats, battered from a night of fighting, rush in, swish their tails, and meow. Maureen coos at them as she gives them fresh water and kibble.

As she sips her coffee, Maureen hears Henry shuffle from the bedroom. She hears his morning splash into the toilet bowl followed by the sound of flushing of water. He honks his nose. Sniffs. Chortles. Maybe he will shave for the party. It's the least he can do, knowing this will probably be their last New Year's Eve here. With three boys sharing a single bedroom, the house is bursting at the seams. The good news is that Henry has a new job at the local meatpacking plant. It's regular work, a union job with benefits. Maureen is hoping they'll soon be able to find a larger place to live.

Remnants of yesterday's argument rise in the back of her throat. Henry ran into Rachel Schuler at the grocery store. He had the audacity—*the audacity*—to invite her to the party. Maureen has barely spoken to Rachel in the three years since she and Henry last hosted the neighbourhood's annual end-of-year get-together. The summer before, Rachel's long-haul-driver husband had left her for a woman ten years his junior living in Saskatoon. At a quarter to midnight, Maureen had slipped upstairs to pee. Peering out the bathroom window after washing her hands, she saw them standing in the shadow that the yellow light from the kitchen window cast from a leafless tree, boots unlaced, jackets wrapped around them. Henry pulled Rachel closer, a beer bottle dangling in his free hand. Biting her lower lip, Maureen inhaled a deep forbearing breath and, almost losing her balance, proceeded back down the stairs. When Henry stumbled into the house a few minutes later, Maureen threw a glare at him. Clueless, he returned his usual droopy-dog, drunken smile. When midnight struck, Maureen turned away from Henry, who was standing expectantly beside her, and instead planted a deep kiss on Jack MacLeod's surprised lips. Maureen held onto that kiss just enough to get Henry's blood boiling—but not enough to start a fight. She then turned to him, scowled, and walked away. Henry shrugged, chugged his beer, and softly belched.

Maureen was standing over the stove, waiting for the water to boil for dinner, when Henry told her about seeing Rachel.

"No harm inviting her, is there?"

"Maybe I'll invite my boyfriend. How about that?"

"Trying to be funny, are you?"

She gave the wooden spoon she held a sharp rap against the pot and turned to him.

"You invited her. Now you can uninvite her."

"No can do."

"How would you like it if I invited some guy you caught me smooching with?"

"Water under the bridge."

"So you've said. For the umpteenth time."

"Doesn't matter. She's living with that Canadian Tire grease monkey, Kevin."

"Ken. Not Kevin. So, what else happened?"

"Nothing."

"That's what you keep saying."

"For fuck's sake. It was years ago. And you still don't believe me," Henry replies, his voice rising. "Besides, she came on to me. We were both drunk. She was…."

"Looking for a roll in the hay with a dead horse? She sure as hell found one."

"At least I didn't invite the neighbourhood dykes."

"Lesbians aren't interested in other women's husbands." With that Maureen walked out of the room.

She recoils at the cold taste of her coffee. As she makes a fresh cup of instant, she listens to the familiar snapping and creaking of Henry coming down the stairs. With each step, Maureen senses the habitual acrimony they share steal down behind him. Over the years, Henry has put a fist through the drywall. He's thrown cups and plates, cursed at her and the boys until he was blue in the face, although, lucky for him, he's never raised a fist to her, or threatened to, even when they've been spitting venom at each other.

As he steps into the kitchen, Maureen places Henry's coffee in its usual place. He sits. Yawns and stretches. Wipes his mouth with the palm of a hand that hasn't touched her in years. Grunting good morning, he brings the cup to his mouth and blows into the steaming brew. They sit across from one another, dull knives scraping at concrete. What started as lust before becoming something called love is now a union that operates on fumes of conspicuous thriftiness as they squeeze what they can from this subarctic prairie city where winters are dark and summers are spent swatting away mosquitoes and blackflies.

A small smile crosses her face. Tom Nicholson has hinted he might drop by at the party.

"What?"

"Nothing," she replies. "It should be fun."

"What?"

"The party."

"Well, if it makes you feel any better, Rachel's not coming. Kevin…"

"Ken…"

"Whatever. He and Rachel are goin' to go to a party with his buds from the shop. Just the mechanics and their wives. No shirts allowed. So there you be."

There you be? Is that all you have to say, she thinks.

=

The Fitzpatricks live on the east side of the city. The sight of teenage girls pushing strollers with newborn babies is not uncommon. Boyfriends—transient and otherwise—and the rare biological father, with mulligan haircuts and unshaven faces, work boots, grease-stained jeans, and black muscle shirts, spend summer weekends drinking rye whiskey from plastic cups. Multitasking is defined by the ability to scratch your balls with one hand, hold a cigarette in the other, and let out a deep belch while peering into the open hood of a beat-up redneck special. Single moms—the luckier ones who have managed to migrate from trailer parks to subsidized rental units—sit on the front steps in rickety aluminum chairs that creak and groan from the extra pounds the years have strapped to their hips. Thin cotton tank tops barely hold back the roll of flesh, little white crescents of tickety-boo butt-cheek press out from too-short cut-off jeans. Beer or coolers in hand, they spend the long evening before dusk smoking, lollygagging, and fighting off the hordes of pesky insects. They offer up a greeting to anyone passing, turn and gaze after an unfamiliar car, possibly driven by a knight in shining armour, that cruises down the street, ready to pick up someone luckier than they are for a night of cheap booze, country music, and desperate sex. Occasionally a mother screaming and swearing at the social workers taking her children away breaks the tedium. Her neighbours fill the silence that follows with a collective "Tsk-tsk, 'tisn't right, but she should've known better."

The streets are lined with identical post-World War II cereal-box houses and nineteen-fifties rental duplexes with stucco, eczema paint, and dented aluminum siding. Weather-beaten plastic pots stand in tiny rectangular yards to suggest that grass might be a long-sought eventuality. In winter, rusting bikes, broken toy dump trucks, and headless dolls hibernate in the snow. The rare picture-perfect house, with a manicured lawn and garden maintained by elderly Ukrainian owners, adds a quiet aesthetic to a neighbourhood where success is measured by a clean criminal record and a steady job. A diploma from a community college is the equivalent of grabbing the brass ring.

Maureen and Henry's rental house is no more than an urban cave that offers shelter from the long frigid winters and the stifling summer heat. When they moved in, they bickered because the landlord offered to reimburse them for any improvements they made. Nothing structural, of course. Just paint and paper.

"I'm not fixing up no goddamn house for no Paki," Henry bellowed.

"He's not a Paki. He's a Sikh."

"He's a taxi-driving turban head. That's what he is. He's probably got what two, three wives… collecting welfare while sitting on his fat taxicab-ass all day."

"At least he owns his house," Maureen replied, sharply.

=

Maureen looks forward to the annual New Year's Eve party. She's gone to enough of them to know they are merely an excuse for everyone to get rip-roaring drunk. For her, it is her once-a-year opportunity to pamper herself. The parties are potluck, BYOB, open-door affairs. Friends and neighbours congregate at a different house each year to drink, chew the fat, dance, and drink some more. Parents leave their kids at home in front of the television or in the care of older siblings, the collective thinking being that, drunkenness aside, it should be easy enough to rescue them should a fire break out. Throughout the night, an underlying current of silent hustle circulates as partygoers— married, single, divorced, happy and unhappy—seek whatever opportunities that present themselves. The odd dustups are never serious enough to call the police because the last thing anyone wants to do is bring the cops around. You never know who might have an outstanding warrant. As midnight nears on the eastern seaboard, the host summons everyone to gather around the television to watch Dick Clark's *New Year's Rockin' Eve* from Times Square. When, three hours early, the clock strikes twelve, wet kisses and drunken hugs are exchanged, followed by a premature and slurred rendition of "Auld Lang Syne."

Henry has gone to the government liquor store, complaining as he pulled on his boots about the long lineups with everyone in the world worried that the liquor commission will run out of booze. Dale, Kenny, and Patrick have settled in front of the television until guests arrive.

As Maureen turns the knob on the bathroom door, she feels suddenly weary. She blinks away the hot flash that courses underneath her eyelids and locks herself in. At times like these, she doesn't give a damn if one of the boys does his business outside against a backyard tree. Slipping into the claw-footed bathtub, with its veneer of chipped enamel, she lies in an embrace of water so hot she clenches her teeth, closes her eyes, and listens to the drone of distant traffic while magpies fight. Water leaks in meditative drips from the tap that Henry has yet to fix. Opening her eyes slightly, she watches hot fog curl upwards in a wisp of angel hair before vanishing into the drafty cold air. She sighs, disappointed in her white legs spread-eagled against the walls of the tub, knowing her body is not, by any stretch of the imagination, a triumph of middle age. Fat sags over her hips. Her pubis perks up above the water, its greying patch skimming the surface. After the water turns tepid, Maureen pulls the plug. A small whirlpool forms around the drain. She wonders if it is true that whirlpools turn counterclockwise in Australia.

She stands in front of the bathroom mirror. She hates staring at her reflection. Her hair clings to her head. Her tired, her *oh-so-tired* face is mottled. Her cheeks are splotched. From the neck down, her skin has turned red. Years of carrying children, flipping mattresses and hoisting trays of beer before she married have rounded her shoulders. She wonders if this is the best it gets, God forbid, it can't get any worse now, can it? It is in private moments like this that separation and divorce cross her mind. Where would she go? What would she do? The poor cannot afford to be apart.

Maureen slips on her worn burgundy bathrobe, woven into a tapestry of pulls and divots from the cats kneading her chest. She reaches for the hair dryer in the bottom drawer of the vanity, wiping off the cylinder with a sheet of toilet paper, just in case the dust sparks up and fills the bathroom with a burning odour.

Lipstick on, she pulls her favourite dress from the closet. She found it years ago on the marked-down rack at Sears. Draping it over her forearm, she goes downstairs and into the living room. The boys' eyes remain fixed on the television. The only evidence they give that indicates she is alive is the irritated look they make at the sound of metal grating on metal as she sets up the ironing board. Patrick looks at her and laughs.

"Whad'ya do with your hair, Mom?"

"Whad'ya do with your brain, Patrick?" she replies smartly.

As she waits for the iron to heat up, Maureen stares at her boys. She wants them to define success however they choose. Live unremarkable. prosperous lives. More than anything, she longs for her sons to become the kind of men who take care of those they love.

She licks her finger and tests the iron. Her saliva sizzles just enough to confirm that it is ready. As she presses her dress, she smiles at Kenny. On Sundays his eyes are glued to the television during *Mutual of Omaha's Wild Kingdom*. He's always exploring the backyard and nearby parks. Sometimes, when she passes the boys' bedroom, she will pause to watch him stare out the window, counting stars, wondering if Martians really exist.

"What do you think, boys?" she asks, holding the freshly pressed dress against her body. "Think your fat momma can still fit into this thing?"

"You're not fat, Mom," Kenny replies. "Just short for your size," he says, ha-ha-ing at his own joke.

She smirks to herself. Ungrateful little bugger. Maureen levers the blunt end of the ironing board to the floor, squeezes the metal clasp, and folds in the legs. The metal runners screech. The boys are united in their annoyance.

"Mommm," they protest in a collective voice.

"You can stay up till nine."

As Maureen passes through the room to go upstairs, she hears the click of the front door. Henry's home. She ignores him by turning her thoughts to Tom Nicholson, the produce manager at the Safeway where Maureen works. Tom has hinted that he might drop in at the party. Maureen met him on her first day on the job, when the store manager was giving her a tour of the sales floor. Tom pressed the box of cantaloupes he was holding against the display counter, swiped a thick, damp hand across his smock, and extended it out to her. "Welcome," he said, his broad smile revealing a slightly crooked front tooth. As the weeks passed, he made a point of asking her how her day was going, how she was doing. He lent a hand whenever he could—like the time she had problems with the scanner. Though his family is out of town for the holidays to visit his wife's mother, who is battling cancer, Maureen doesn't have a clue why Tom would be interested in coming to this part of the city on his own time. Hell, the only reason he even comes to the neighbourhood is for work. Still, she supposes it beats ringing in the New Year alone, but surely he must have a more hoity-toity party to go to.

She sits on the bed that she and Henry share and stares at the two yellow foam earplugs in her jewellery bowl. She can't bear to throw them out. They are souvenirs from when she took everyone to Monster Jam at the Coliseum. They spent the night watching modified pickup trucks, with names like Grave Digger and King Krunch, race around the arena. Truth be known, she was tired from work and bored as hell but nevertheless put on a brave mom face and watched, pleased, as the boys sat on the edge of their nosebleed seats and stared wide-eyed as trucks spewed out smoke and fire, roared around on ten-foot tires, crushed cars, did doughnuts, wheelies, and aerial flips over artificial sand dunes while the boisterous blue-collar crowd—egged on by beer and big-breasted twenty-year-old women in tight-fitting cheerleader costumes—went wild. The ear plugs—at a dollar a pop—offered little protection from the relentless sonic booms that ricocheted off the coliseum walls and ceiling. Maureen sipped on a overpriced soft drink as the boys gorged on hot dogs and soft drinks and Henry filled his belly with beer. She went home with a headache and ringing ears.

It was the happiest she had felt in years.

Weeks after Monster Jam, Maureen confided in Tom about her next project. She wanted to take Henry and the boys to Disneyland. She'd need at least a year, if not longer, to set enough money aside. She told Tom that she dare not tell Henry of her plans. He'd argue that the money would be better spent on things like new brakes on the car.

"You can never be too old for Disney," he replied with a smile.

She stands in front of the bed and slips the dress over her head. Sleeveless, hemmed respectably below the knee, it is a contrast to the slippers that Maureen's wearing. They are worn, but functional, and keep her warm during the winter. She watches out of the corner of her eye as Henry steps into the room. He changes into a pair of corduroys and the only dress shirt he owns. He tucks it in, stands behind Maureen, and gazes into an empty spot in the mirror. He runs his hand through his hair, over his shoulders and pecs, checks to ensure that the shirt's two top buttons are open at the neck before sitting down on his side of the bed. He reaches for his shoes and wipes off the dust with his hand as Maureen pulls a tube of lipstick from the bedside table.

"Well, well, aren't we trying to be fancy tonight," he says with a wink, stomping the heel of his shoe into the floor and walking out into the hall.

From the back of the closet, Maureen pulls a shoebox, lifts the lid, and smiles at the pair of black shoes with low heels she'd bought recently bought at a clearance sale at Army and Navy. She carefully peels the sales tag off the heel and crumples it in her hand. While slipping the shoes on, she hears Henry in the kitchen below as he goes on about something or other. Maureen shakes her head and, concluding that if love is a summer breeze, marriage is a winter storm.

=

The night sky is salted with stars. Bundled up in thick coats, parkas, and heavy winter boots, friends and neighbours arrive in pairs and small groups, each laden with beer and mickeys in brown bags. A few thick-skulled louts arrive, having braved the frigid air with open jackets and shirts, chest muscles flexed. As they get out of their cars and trucks, Maureen and Henry greet them warmly from the front steps, warning them to be careful as they make their way up the walk. Most of the women arrive at the party assuming the men have the collective objective of getting as drunk as they can in the shortest time possible. The women too will drink. Some more than others. Underlying this is expectation that it is the women who will get their men home safely.

The boys take turns sneaking potato chips and Cheezies from the snack bowls, coating their hands in a greasy paste from the orange puff chips. Filling their mouths, the boys laugh excitedly as they drift to the male side of the party and watch as cigarette ashes are flicked into empty beer bottles. They listen to talk about all things manly, cars, women, sports, flatulence: three in a row is a hat trick, four is a home run; blame the silent-but-deadlies on the non-existent dog. Nancy Black's newest boyfriend or latest date—Maureen can't keep track—tries to impress Patrick by sticking a lit cigarette up his nose. The stranger inhales, coughs spastically, and turns red in the face while everyone around him breaks out in laughter. Unsurprisingly, Samantha Washington is the most irritating person at the party. She has a smoker's voice and cackles at the slightest provocation. Her hoots carry through the kitchen.

The lesbians are the last to arrive. Lucy and Molly come bearing two bottles of something French that Maureen doesn't even try to pronounce. They're nice. Neighbourly. Lucy brought a casserole over when the Fitzpatricks moved in two years ago. Henry keeps them at a polite distance. As if one's sexual preference were contagious. He's not a religious guy, but when he found out Lucy and Molly were a couple, he quickly pointed out that if God had intended women to sleep together, he wouldn't have given men a penis. And if men didn't have a penis, Maureen responded curtly, they wouldn't have a thing to play with.

Lucy is Jennifer's mother. The fact that her mother left Jennifer's father for Molly is of no concern to Maureen. Jennifer is one of Patrick's best friends. She holds her own during road-hockey games and is known to give—and take—an elbow. She excels at basketball and, if she keeps it up, has been told that she might even be able to play college ball. Most important, Jennifer is a foil to Lance Moore. Lance is also Patrick's road-hockey buddy and friend. Maureen sees no good in Lance, predicting he will end up in juvie detention—just like his older brother.

Not before long, the windows begin to sweat from heat colliding with the cold outside. The women stand in small groups, drinks in hand. Some hold their glasses. Others smoke their cigarettes and pose, lifting their heads to blow smoke toward the ceiling. They gossip, regurgitate headlines from the grocery-store tabloids while catching up on the latest neighbourhood scuttlebutt: welfare visited Sara Jones for the second time this month; an ambulance took old Mrs. Grabowski away and she's not been seen since; Maude Hunter won $200 at the bingo.

Floating between kitchen and living room, Maureen does her best to ignore the partiers who huddle on the back deck and pass around the green herb. The air around them is so thick with fog and smoke you can almost touch it. She makes a point of chatting with Lucy and Molly, making sure they are comfortable. Maureen watches the men with caution. Some gaze at the couple, bewildered that a pretty woman like Lucy now bats for the other side. Maureen sees Joe Black leaning against the windowsill, his eyes narrow and unblinking. There has always been something unsettling about him. Joe slowly peels the corner of the label off this beer bottle and rubs it absentmindedly between his fingers. Surely, for god's sake, he can't feel threatened, Maureen thinks. Even after bearing him three kids, Melinda, who works in the ladies' department at Sears, is a woman no man would kick out of bed for eating crackers. Joe winks to Maureen as he takes a long pull on his beer. She wonders if he'd caught her watching him.

"How's it going, Joe?"

"Fine, Maureen. Just fine."

"I think your wife might need a refill. What you think?"

"Good idea," he replies and saunters into the kitchen.

Maureen sees Lucy and Molly more as soft lesbian/hard lesbian, good lesbian/bad lesbian. Lucy, the younger of the two, with her Nordic roots and long blonde hair and large white teeth, does not look like what Maureen pictures a lesbian to be. Lucy charms everyone in sight, breezing in and out of conversations while effortlessly offering tidbits of social commentary. If Lucy is the poster girl for lipstick lesbians, the older Molly epitomizes the surly butch dyke. She works in the parts department at a car dealership, wears her dyed-black hair short, and always seems to have a hardened scowl on her face—as if every second of every day she has something to prove. Molly is a ballsy woman, having succeeded with a human rights claim against a local men's recreation hockey league after they refused to let her play because she was a woman. Henry has speculated that Molly probably has a tattoo—a coiled viper, mouth wide open, fangs bared—inked between her legs. While he won't admit it, Henry is grateful that she and Lucy make a point of keeping an eye on Patrick whenever he and Maureen have to work late.

The house is liquored up and the party firing on all cylinders when Maureen answers the door. Tom Nicholson holds out a bottle of wine.

"I thought I would take you up on your offer."

"Come in."

There is an awkward pause.

Although he'd said he might drop by, Maureen is still surprised. He leans in as if to kiss her. Instead, he presses a hand on the doorsill and bends at the waist. Grunting, Tom tugs off his boots. Maureen inhales his breath—a combination of peppermint and cigarette smoke. He's told her that, lung cancer be damned, he likes his cigarettes. He's complained to her about head office frowning on employees smelling of cigarette smoke while working, especially around produce—as if a smoker's breath can somehow defile the carrots, peppers, and onions.

He reaches inside his jacket.

"I got a little something for you."

Tom pulls out a dog-eared booklet, *A Pictorial Souvenir of Walt Disney's Disneyland.*

"For your trip."

"Why, thank you."

"We have no use for it. The kids are past the Disney stage. They're more at the Cancun-all-inclusive phase of life."

"You're sure?"

"Of course."

Maureen stares at the front cover. White fissures of wear cut into a page-sized glossy image of the world-famous magical castle. As she flicks through, a kaleidoscope of all things Disney glitters before her eyes: the bronze statue of Walt Disney, Mickey and Goofy posing for the camera, The Mad Hatter Shop, Main Street U.S.A.

"The key is to plan your trip ahead of time. I can help if you like. Before you go, sit down with the boys and figure out what their top rides are for each day and go from there." He motions to the book. "I'd hide that if I were you. You don't want to spoil the surprise now, do you?"

"I've got a ways to go yet."

"I just hope things don't go sideways for you."

"Sideways?"

He shrugs his shoulders.

Maureen slips the book into the back of the top shelf of the hallway closet. Turning, Maureen comes face to face with Tom and resists the sudden, inexplicable urge to pull him into her. A vision flashes before her—of Maureen taking Tom upstairs to Henry's and her bedroom where they will fuck. Hell, she thinks with an absurd grin, maybe they will do it right in the middle of the living room. What would Henry think? The party guests? Tom and Maureen whipping their clothes off, rolling around with everyone cheering them on, eager for the chance to join in. That would make for one helluva New Year's Eve party, now wouldn't it?

"What?" Tom asks.

"Nothing. I just had a thought."

"Must've been a good one."

"I think I need to get us both a drink."

Maureen blushes when she accidentally touches Tom's hand with her finger. As they cross the living room, Maureen drops her hand to her side. Guests, drunk, wary, give the newcomer the once-over. Tom's dress pants and pressed white shirt with its thin blue and black vertical strips confirms that he's not from around here.

"Henry, remember Tom?"

"Course I do." Henry nods to the kitchen. "Beer's in the fridge. Help yourself." He turns his back and rejoins his friends in conversation. Henry has always remained standoffish with Tom, despite Maureen telling Henry that he was once a card-carrying union man.

"Was," Henry replied. "Now his job is to turn the screws on the rank and file. Squeeze 'em till they bleed. Just like all the other white shirts."

"Someone's got to manage the place."

"How hard can it be?" Henry scoffed "Managing a glorified vegetable stand? Loading asparagus and melons? Coordinating three full-time and five part-time staff? He wouldn't last an hour at the plant."

Maureen introduces Tom to the boys. They are awkward in their politeness, the introduction a temporary interruption in their quest for more treats. They wipe their hands on their jeans and shake the one he extends. She leads Tom into the kitchen, averting her eyes from the stares of the more curious guests, knowing that Tom's presence will only add to the post-party neighbourhood gossip. Despite spending the morning cleaning and scrubbing, Maureen is suddenly self-conscious, embarrassed at what Tom sees: chipped and bubbled paint, a faded Formica kitchen table, water taps as old as the house itself.

"It's got good bones," he says, looking around as if sensing her anxiety. "Good solid bones."

She imagines his house having the picture-perfect touches in the magazine spreads she sometimes scans during breaks at work. She's always found Tom to be a bit out of place, as if he's too smart to have ended up working at a supermarket. Why has he come to their party? she wonders. To this dump on the wrong side of the city? To make himself feel superior? No, that's not like him, she tells herself.

"Corkscrew?" Tom asks, tapping the top of the bottle with his finger.

Maureen searches in the utensil drawer. She curses the boys under her breath as her hand barely misses the sharp edge of an upturned knife. She digs to the bottom of the drawer and extracts the rarely used wine opener. Tom accepts it with a smile. Maureen watches as he expertly twists in the corkscrew, each turn as sturdy as it is strong. He flexes his wrists, presses down on the rabbit-eared handles, and leverages the cork from the bottle.

"It's a Syrah. From Australia."

Maureen only knows wine as either red or white.

Tom rolls the cork in his hand. Examines it. He sniffs the mouth of the dark green bottle and pours into the glasses sitting on the counter.

He hands Maureen her glass. Raises his. The kitchen light barely penetrates the deep red liquid. It makes Maureen think of the blood of Jesus. They smile and toast without exchanging a word. She sips slowly, supposing that wine, like beer and hard liquor, is an acquired taste. They remain in the kitchen. Talk mainly of work, oblivious to the partygoers around them. The more he speaks, the more Maureen is convinced Tom is flirting with her. She looks through the kitchen doorway. Henry stares at them with a sour gaze.

"I…" she begins, motioning towards the living room.

"Understand," he says. "After all, you're the hostess with the mostess."

=

It is after two when the last guest rags out the door. The kitchen counters and table are covered with empty bottles and cans. Mounds of grey ash and cigarette butts fill ashtrays. The sink is stacked high with dirty dishes. The linoleum is coated with a sticky sheen. Maureen pulls a large plastic garbage bag from under the sink. The stale sickly smell awakens her senses.

"Leave it," Henry orders, his voice gruff from drink. "The boys can help in the morning."

The bag flutters to the floor.

She follows him upstairs and into bed. She turns off her light and stares at the black ceiling unable to sleep.

"Whatcha doing kissing your boss for?" Henry asks.

"One, he's not my boss. He's the produce manager. And two, I didn't kiss him. He kissed me."

"Doesn't matter."

"It's what people do at midnight."

"How would you like it if…"

"Don't even go there."

The next morning, Maureen wakes to the sound of dishes rattling and bottles banging. Muffled voices echo from the kitchen below. Feeling sour from the late night, she makes her way down the stairs, gripping the railing, hands shaky. Henry, clearly suffering from an even more calamitous hangover and still in his pyjamas, is on his hands and knees on the kitchen floor, one hand bracing himself, the other in a bucket of soapy grey water.

"Thought we'd let you sleep in," he says, his voice raspy.

Patrick holds open a large green garbage bag as Dale swipes his forearm across the kitchen table, snowplowing empty plastic cups and paper napkins over the edge and into the bag.

"Mom, look," Kenny cries out, pointing to the stack of beer cans and liquor bottles beside the back door. "Dad says we can keep the money."

"Only if you finish cleaning up," Henry says.

"Many hands make for small work," Maureen quips. She rubs her hands against her nightie before turning on the taps to fill up the sink with hot water.

While they wash and dry, Maureen skilfully probes Henry with questions that might expose any hard feelings that he may have from the night before.

A little while later, she takes the Disney book upstairs to the bedroom and closes the door. Sitting on the side of the bed, she flips through it. When she reaches the last page, she stares at a stickie note with a phone number pencilled with Tom's handwriting.

You're kidding, Maureen says to herself, breaking into a smile.

She continues to stare at the numbers, wondering, Tom, what in God's name?

Maureen closes the book and presses it to her chest before slipping it into the back of her bedside drawer. She has other matters to attend to, the most pressing being the annual family New Year's Day breakfast.

Already the boys are calling up the stairs and asking when she's going to start making bacon, eggs, and pancakes with syrup, plenty of sweet Aunt Jemima syrup.

# FREE RANGE

Maureen was nineteen and slinging beer at the Black Gold Hotel when they met. Six months before she had hightailed it four hours south by Greyhound bus to this dull, conservative city with its small downtown and cookie-cutter suburbs that blanket the prairie landscape as far as the eye can see. She'd been hoping to someday finish her high-school diploma, maybe become a nurse's aide. Things just didn't work out that way.

Henry was twenty, working as a labourer when he saw her. She blushed each time she served him, especially when he told her she was as pretty as apple pie. "And I like apple pie," he quipped with a drunken smile. It was the sort of flirting that waitresses expect—just enough to catch the attention of the bouncers. Lucky for Henry, Maureen caught their eye before they could come over and make mincemeat of him. She agreed to meet him for coffee. He quickly cooed her into his bed.

As they lay beside each other, sharing a cigarette, he told her that he loved her. That was enough for her. Dancing, drinking, and plenty of sex filled their time. When she found out she was pregnant, Maureen was all set to move back home, her tail between her legs. Henry caught her flatfooted by asking her to marry him. She wrote her mother to invite her to the civil ceremony in the city, but she declined, saying coming down would interfere with her bingo night.

What Henry offered Maureen was a roof over her head and, during the early years of their marriage, a happiness she had never felt before. Nor would she ever feel again. At an early age, having been told to believe in God and play by the rules, they knew to seek nothing more than life's basic pleasures. They were too ignorant to realize how the deck was stacked against them: the sole purpose of their union was to produce the next generation of themselves. They started having terrible arguments late into the night, said terrible things, declared their hatred for one another in between the slamming of doors and threats to leave. Inevitably, they would end up in bed, where the world was warm and wonderful.

In addition to giving birth to Dale, Kenny, and Patrick, Maureen miscarried twice. Both were girls. The second girl died inside her and she was forced to carry the baby for two months until she could have a normal birth. She later wondered if her drinking and smoking—though she drank very little while pregnant and smoked only at social gatherings or while having a drink—was the cause of the miscarriages. Gradually, she set her mind at ease, concluding it was no more than bad luck. Or bad genes. What the miscarriages did teach Maureen was not to be afraid of death.

It wasn't long after Kenny was born that Maureen began to feel the love from the one she hoped would always bring it begin to fade. The family grew, moved frequently before settling into a rental house within walking distance of the river valley. The dog they brought with them promptly got killed by a car and was replaced by a pair of goldfish that Henry referred to as Flush One and Flush Two. They would eventually settle on two SPCA cats.

Time worked on Henry. He turned into a gruff man with eyes that became more menacing with age. His hands were thick, his palms calloused, fingers peppered with nicks and scars. He'd worked with his back his whole life and carried barely an ounce of fat on his body. He combed his black, greased hair back, furrowed it to one side.. On most weekends and the occasional holiday—out of sheer laziness—he'd skip shaving, his salt-and-pepper stubble reminiscent of black-and-white pictures of Wild West gunfighters, their faces taut, eyes gleaming with intent to take down their next quarry. His deep-seated anger and need to lash out, which came with his drinking, were familiar to Maureen, but they were more than offset by lighthearted, melancholic drunken admissions of abiding love for her because, for the most part, Henry was a happy-go-lucky drunk—unless too much alcohol triggered something deeper inside of him. The fear he'd strike impulsively, vigorously, and without mercy, just as he had when he was a young roadhouse brawler, lingered around the house. When he drank a lot Henry could always find something to gripe about, something to be angry with. There was always something—a story in the newspaper, politicians, potholes. The weather. Rising gas prices. Or he'd traipse around the house looking for something out of place; a jacket on the floor, winter boots blocking the door.

Henry learned from a young age that real men worked with their hands, not their heads, respect was earned with fists and boots, not brains and books, and that their true measure was found in their toughness. From the moment he held Dale in his arms, he was determined that his son would follow in his footsteps. He would not become a barber. Or a hairdresser. Dale, and the two that followed, would not work in a flower shop, a card store, or God forbid, the makeup department at Sears. They would not even think about becoming lawyers or doctors because law and medicine took brains and money. He would discourage them from becoming preachers or politicians because the only thing worse than a politician was a lawyer who became a politician or preacher who morphed into a pedophile.

For Dale's ninth birthday, Henry gave him a pair of boxing gloves. Dale stood barefoot in the living room, arms limp, knees weak. A sleeveless T-shirt drooped over the gym shorts his father had ordered him to put on. Henry pushed the window open, allowing a hot, dry summer breeze to blow through the room. As he pulled the gloves over his son's small hands, sweat began to layer on Dale's forehead and bead down the side of his small face.

"I'm just gonna give ya a quick lesson," Henry whispered into Dale's ear as he lashed the long white laces about Dale's wrists, his breath a mixture of coffee and cigarettes.

Dale looked helplessly at his mother, who stood stooped over the empty kitchen sink. Her lower lip quivered. Her arms trembled as she twisted at the waist just enough to make eye contact with Dale, in her eyes the look of a mother waiting for a child's broken bone to be set.

Henry stepped back, pride etched on his face. "Maybe later on, we'll take you down to the boxing club. Sign you up." He held up a finger. "Lesson number one. Never fight a redskin. They'll just as soon stick a knife in your back as buy you a beer," he said before turning philosophical. "I guess if I'd been sent to some residential school with priests molesting me, I'd be pretty pissed too."

He stared intently at Dale, his eyes narrowing. Dale pulled the gloves protectively over his face. Henry winked. "Number two…" He feigned a bob, a weave, and a short jab. He stopped, suddenly serious, his unshaven face almost touching Dale's pink skin. "You don't pick a fight. Got it? But you never—*never*—back down from one either." Henry rose. He pressed out his chest. "The key is to get in the first punch. Do you hear?" He stepped back and playfully slap-slap-slapped Dale's gloves with his fingers. "Watch his eyes. And when he blinks." Henry thrust a right uppercut into the air. "Kapow."

Dale blinked. Henry responded with a sharp poke to the ribs and a jab that stopped barely an inch from the boy's face. He reflexively cringed. Curled forward at the waist, tears in the corners of his eyes. "Gotcha, didn't I?" Dale straightened up and dropped his left hand. Henry flicked Dale's nose with his middle finger. Dale ran, crying, into the kitchen, a trickle of blood leaking from his nose.

"That's enough," Maureen hollered.

"Crying won't make him a man, ya hear? Come on back. I won't hurt you. Promise,"

"Touch him again and…."

"What?"

"You'll not be using your son as a punching bag. Not Dale. Nor the other boys. Got it? No more bloody noses, for Chrissake. He just turned nine. Nonna that on Patrick. And if you lift a finger to Kenny, there'll be hell to pay."

"You're not going to be around to protect them their whole lives now, will ya?" he fumed, his words a prescient foreboding.

"Maybe not. But I'll be here for them till the day I die."

They argued as Dale watched safely from behind his mother's legs, his eyes darting from his bloody fingers to his father's face. It was then that he vowed to never let his father touch him again.

The next garbage day, Maureen threw the gloves into the bin.

=

Dale was twelve when the family moved, for the last time, to a house three blocks from the river valley. The house brimmed with testosterone, sweat, and everything male. Fighting was as natural as breathing. Blood spilled. Bones broke. Open wounds were stitched closed. Over the years, Maureen lost count of the number of visits she made to the Royal Alex's emergency room with one of the boys or took a phone call from the school. As brother-versus-brother battles increased in frequency, Maureen became more of a referee than a mother. Exhausted from yet again separating two of her sons, she once told Henry that miscarrying might have been a blessing, for she could see no good in bringing girls into this house.

The boys nonetheless had an unyielding love for their mother. There was something in the way this rough woman who was prone to mood swings—one moment melancholy, laughing the next—found solace in her sons and they in her. Yet when implausible words and phrases —"be happy," "hope for the best," "don't give up"— came out of her mouth, the boys would roll their eyes. The absurdity of her optimism was summarized by a poster that Dale hung up in his basement bedroom during his teenage years. It was of a bright yellow happy face with a downturned smile and the word *Shit* italicized underneath.

They'd become free-range boys, roaming the neighbourhood and the river valley at will, passing the time watching television at a friend's house, playing Pacman, doing what they pleased as long as they were home for dinner, and later, after dinner, when the streetlights came on. Their territory was a working-class neighbourhood bordered by the Yellowhead Highway to the north and the North Saskatchewan River to the south. In the distance, refinery row and its industrial swamp dominated the eastern sky with red and white smokestacks that spewed steam and poison high into the air. But they were oblivious, carefree anad happy. Happiness had nothing to do with hope. Hope was found in a weekly lottery ticket, success an apprenticeship or a steady job in the oil patch.

Kenny is three years younger than Dale. He is the quiet one, which makes his brothers suspicious of him, nervous because he is different. He's a scrawny boy, his small size perhaps the result of him being born premature, his top-heavy head a sort of mini version of Edvard Munch's *The Scream*. This makes his ears appear larger than they are. His uneven front teeth are offset by a pair of deep blue eyes. As uncoordinated as all nine-year-old boys are, Kenny has retained just enough of his public-school innocence to be confused by the shy smiles of girls when they look at him. He suffers from asthma. The attacks are scary to see—his lungs desperately sucking in the last molecules of oxygen from the air before his mother hands him his puffer and rubs his back until the medication kicks in. *"It's okay. It's okay. Try to breathe normal. That's it. Deep breaths."* When the doctor suggests Henry refrain from smoking inside the house, he moves the ashtray to the chair beside the window. When he lights up, he cracks the window open no more than the width of the glowing red tip of his cigarette. He exhales plumes of hissing grey smoke through the opening that the outside air pushes back in.

At seven, Patrick is the youngest of the trio. With an impish ignorance that matches his equally goofy grin, he is an unassuming boy, still too young to have either focus or purpose. His arms are thin and he has the unfortunate habit of picking his nose at the most inappropriate times. All Patrick ever wants for Christmas and birthday is enough new Hot Wheels tracks so he can send his cars screaming down the stairs through a full loop at the bottom— just like in the commercials—before they crash safely into a pillow propped up against the wall. When he told his parents that he wanted to be a stunt driver, Maureen reminded him that even stunt drivers need a high-school diploma while Henry suggested he might consider becoming a mechanic instead. On winter nights, he spends his time watching *Degrassi High*, *The Simpsons*, or *Hockey Night in Canada* with the cats curled up beside him. Otherwise, he's immersed in Hardy Boys mysteries, his comic books, or he's outside playing shinny with friends, wielding a hockey stick that has a pencil-thin blade.

Fights between the younger brothers break out with great regularity. That is, until the day they accidentally hit their mother. They are in the kitchen, fighting about who has first dibs on the peanut butter, each so focused on the other that neither hears their mother approach. She steps between them and ends up flat on her back. The boys kneel down and stare at her, each blaming the other, uncertain who had thrown the offending punch.

She slowly gets to her feet, adjusts herself, and staggers to a kitchen chair.

"I'm so sorry, boys. I must've slipped."

Maureen never does tell Henry the truth about the red welt on her face.

Dale is bigger, stronger, and more mature. This does not prevent him from egging on his brothers mercilessly, for this is what older brothers are destined to do. He does this with the understanding that when he pushes it too far, he tempts the wrath of his parents. He learned the hard way the time he took his playfighting too far the summer before Kenny drowned. Dale and Patrick were wrestling in the backyard and he accidentally elbowed Patrick in the face. It was only a glancing blow but enough to draw blood and, quickly, tears. Patrick stared wide-eyed as blood trickled down his chin and pooled in the palm of his hand. More from the sight of the blood than the actual injury, he burst into tears, wailed, and ran into the house. Almost immediately, Henry stormed out the back door.

"What the hell did you do?"

"I didn't mean too. It was an accident."

"An accident?"

"We were play fighting."

"Like this?" Henry pushed his hands down on Dale's right shoulder, forcing him to the ground. "How do you like it?" He towered over his son. Sneered as Dale crab-walked away on elbows and heels before flipping to his feet and sprinting out onto the street, not to return until after dark.

=

Things have been looking up for Henry. He's been at the plant for three years now. It's a union shop. Not that it really matters because he's only paid a bit above minimum wage—barely enough to cover union dues. But the work is steady. He was promoted to stun-gun operator. Eight hours a day with a half-hour for lunch, five days a week, in the sun, the rain, and the snow, he operates a pneumatic bolt gun. On average, he processes two hundred livestock a day. He gets a bit more money than the line workers because he kills for a living and walks around the plant aware of having a certain prestige. Not everyone has licence to kill for a living. He's learned to shut out the plaintive bawl of the animals as they are prodded up the chute and has discovered that cattle and hogs react differently when a bolt enters their brains. With cattle, the neck contracts in a series of spasms. Hogs collapse in violent convulsions, wheezing, gasping, and gagging.

Some days, though, when Henry catches his reflection in the big brown eyes of a doomed animal, all he sees is death. Out of pity he may scratch a frightened cow behind its ear or rub his knuckles down the back of its skull, whispering into its ear that it is going to be all right before pressing the barrel into position and squeezing the trigger, recoiling as a thousand pounds of triple grade "A" meat, bone, and blood thud to the ground. Though he'd never admit it, he knows the work has killed something inside of him. Has numbed him.

Years later Henry would admit to his sons that he didn't actually kill the animals. Saying he killed just sounded so much more manly. Do you kill for a living? Or merely stun them? He'd reason it's all smoke and mirrors anyway. They were all dead meat. A bolt through the skull would render the cow unconscious, thus preserving the quality of the beef. A labourer would next wrap a chain around the hind legs, before hoisting the animal into the air where a slaughterer—the real killer—clean slashed the animal's throat, allowing it to bleed out. The carcass cooled for twenty-four hours before its magical transformation into lunch-bag and dinner-table cuts began. Henry would emphasize, his voice low, that he always did his best to ensure no animals suffered, reasoning it was their fate to be killed, processed, and consumed.

Henry's drinking peaks every second Friday, payday. At beer o'clock, as he calls it, he saunters to the tavern across the street from the plant and ends up coming home intoxicated enough to inevitably ignite fireworks that much sooner, that much brighter. Maureen often tries to divert his bubbling anger by offering to join him in a game of cards in the kitchen. Whatever the boys are watching on television becomes competition for what is going on in the kitchen—Henry's boisterous voice muttering and cursing whenever he loses a hand he is certain he should've won. *Goddamn*, he shouts, tossing his cards onto the table. The more Maureen and Henry drink, the nastier things get—*shit, fuck, bitch (shh, the boys'll hear you!)*. Mooned by the black-and-white shadows cast by the television, the boys sink into the couch, filtering out the f'ing thises and f'ing thats their father's mouth spits. On nights like this, the house shakes with the potential for things to get out of hand without a moment's notice. It is during one of these card games that the boys hear their mother scream that if she ever won the Lotto, she'd buy their father a one-way ticket to some small island in the Pacific Ocean where he can spend the rest of his life despising the person he hates the most.

Some nights, Henry saunters from the kitchen and into the living room, drink in one hand, the other akimbo on his hip, a gunslinger grin on his face. He stares at the boys. "Whenever's one of you wants to have a go, just let me know," he leers, laughing at his cruel poetry, his eyes fixed on Dale for an extra second. Maureen has always felt that by reining in Dale, Henry thinks he will somehow be able to keep a handle on their two other sons as well.

Maureen has an ace up her sleeve and Henry knows she won't hesitate to use it. All she needs to do is pick up the phone, mention his name and the police will come, lights flashing. They will whisk him away, rough him up a bit on the way to the drunk tank or a nearby motel. The threat is usually enough to shut him up.

As tempers continue to flare in the kitchen, the boys know it is time to head upstairs. As they lie in their beds, the sound of chairs scraping against linoleum and of angry voices thick with idle threats and accusations—*Shut your pie hole... Oh, shut yours yourself, you drunk*—lulls them to sleep.

Sometimes Patrick lies awake on his top bunk in the bedroom he shares with Kenny. One sleepless night he hears his father tell his mother that he wouldn't be in this pickle if she'd taken the proper precautions.

The ebb and flow of resentments screamed from below continues until someone retreats to the living room or Henry passes out. Patrick sometimes hears his father's laboured breathing as Maureen helps him up the stairs. His rank liquored burps drift under the bedroom door. The silence that follows is broken by the purr of a passing vehicle on the street, the intermittent creaking of strained bedsprings, muffled snoring, and the occasional sputter of heavy flatulence.

=

The boys find refuge in the boreal forest that canopies the river valley. It is a refuge brimming with wildlife. Maureen has warned the boys about the dangers: the rabid coyotes, the deer mice and the hantavirus they carry, the pedophiles who troll the woods. Kenny tells his mother that her sons aren't in the habit of sniffing mouse poo, that rabid animals avoid human contact, and their family lives far enough away from the downtown pervs.

The youngest two brothers often hang out in a fort back from the riverbank. Dale and his friends built the fort, then moved on to more mischievous endeavours. It is far enough in the bushes to skirt the scrutiny of, and the destruction by, city staff, yet close enough to the bank that Kenny and Patrick can sit and listen to the rushing water, the cooing of lovers, and families talking as they walk along the path. Its construction is primitive, branches of dead trees over a plastic tarp that is tied down with rope anchored by two logs doubling as seats. A rusting camp stove Dale had pilfered from the scout troop he belonged to sheds warmth during the bitter winter days when they seek refuge from their father. Dale didn't stay long with the scout troop. He was kicked out for telling the scout leader to fuck off. Years later, the same scout leader went to prison for molesting boys. It is here, Dale reveals years later, that he will lose his virginity one summer night. The fort is where Patrick will slip his hand under a girl's bra for the first time and feel the hardening of her nipple, where on a different night he will slither his hand inside the same girl's jeans and afterwards sniff his middle finger to inhale the magic fragrance of a woman for the first time. The fort is also where Patrick, like his oldest brother, will experience the rite of passage of every Canadian boy—the carving of his initials into the snow while emptying his beer-filled bladder while tilting his head toward the stars.

Kenny is most at home in the woods. He's not the Daniel Boone type, scouting around with a coon cap, looking to hunt and trap. He's more a John Audubon or Charles Darwin explorer type and has told his mother that when he grows up he wants to work in Banff or Jasper National Park as a park warden. Maureen imagines him greeting visitors with an outdoorsy smile, offering up a wealth of welcoming news, telling visitors about the greatest show on earth—the elk and the bears, the bighorn sheep and the wolves, that roam the park. Kenny regularly explores the valley with his oversized orange backpack with a blue aluminum frame that he convinced his mother to buy at the Salvation Army. The frame arches across his small buttocks. He traipses down to the river's edge, lifts rocks, peers into holes, and scavenges whatever treasure catches his attention. He brings home skulls and bones, speckled rocks, insects, grasshoppers, and crickets that he tries to keep alive on water and white bread inside glass-jar prisons, as if he were setting up his own miniature science lab or museum display.

During the summer he lays everything out on a wooden pallet that has been sitting in the corner of the backyard since they moved in. One day Dale comes home with a worn white lab coat and a pair of safety glasses. No questions are asked about where they came from. Kenny can now play the real scientist. During the long nights of June, he can often be found on his stomach inches from his latest prized catch—a jar brimming with fireflies. Oblivious to the mosquitoes and blackflies that hover around him, Kenny watches, mesmerized, as the fireflies light up the jar with their tails that beat with an illuminous insect Morse code until his mother calls him in.

When the summer heat gets the better of his collection, Maureen will order Kenny to dispose of the source of the rotting smell, only for him to start all over again. She often stands at the kitchen window beaming with pride at Kenny's curiosity.

"Maybe he'll be a teacher," she tells Henry.

"Maybe he'll drive a truck," he replies dryly, flicking the ashes from his cigarette into the ashtray.

=

Years later, after Patrick is on his own, he wonders if his father's meanness—he can't think of another way to describe it—was in part the result of working around death all day. His father wasn't born mean-spirited. He didn't grow up killing cats or setting sheds on fire. Patrick can never forget the time he came home, tears streaming from his eyes. He had cut his knee in a fall. Henry sat him down in a chair in the kitchen, reached into the refrigerator freezer, and pulled out a Popsicle before attending to the wound. He dabbed away the blood, leaned back in his kitchen chair, hand on his jaw, and assessed the damage. He warned Patrick that this would sting a bit and let him grip his outstretched hand while applying the Ozonol. "*This might require an ice cream. What do ya think?*" Later, as they sat outside on the picnic table next to the neighbourhood Dairy Queen, cones in hand, Henry let Patrick in on a secret. After school was over, they were going to The Calgary Stampede—the Greatest Show on Earth.

=

Now that Dale has reached high-school age, Maureen tries, without much success, to take the brunt of his teenage logic in stride. She worries about the vampire hours he is starting to keep and cannot comprehend his adolescent lunacies. He is oblivious to the risks that accompany his daily idiocies. Maureen attributes them to testosterone. She grudgingly accepts his questionable friends and the time they waste drooling over cars and other nonsense, all at the expense of more important things like school. He has a hormone-fuelled curiosity in girls, and possibly, beer and soft drugs. Academics have never been Dale's strong point. All Maureen can do is hope for the best, knowing that Dale is in so many ways the quintessential big brother, wavering between picking on Kenny and Patrick and doing what their father cannot. Protect them.

He already has a reputation at school. Last term a boy two years his senior challenged Dale to a fight. When the boy blinked, he hit him with a left jab, followed with a right roundhouse and ended the fight with a swift kick to the boy's groin. A three-day suspension followed. Henry phoned the school principal to protest that Dale was only standing up for himself. He slammed down the phone, stormed down into Dale's basement bedroom, and offered him a congratulatory wink. No one tested Dale at school again.

Just before Christmas, while gathering the laundry in his room in the basement—he likes to keep it dark because dark is cool—Maureen found a *Penthouse* under his mattress. She sat on the edge of the bed, held the centrefold at arm's length, and dissed the lithesome girl with the Barbie doll smile and rocket-sized breasts—airbrushed to perfection—with a mother's *tsk-tsk*. She chuckled when she read that the girl hailed from a small town on Vancouver Island. Pamela Anderson was her name. She returned the magazine to its rightful place, finished picking up Dale's laundry, and walked out of the room.

There are times now when Dale will sit in his father's man chair for no more of a reason than to spite him. The chair is positioned between the entrance to the kitchen and the stairs leading to the second floor. It allows Dale to watch television while gauging his father's growing anger in the kitchen. He remains there until he is scooched out with a terse nod of Henry's head. If he doesn't move quick enough, he gets a sharp slap across the knee. Dale responds with eyes full of contempt, knowing the day will come when he will be strong enough to swallow back his fear, confront his father, and pummel him into the carpet. He will hurt him. Kick him in the ribs until they break. Hit him until blood flows from his ears.

=

It is still dark when Henry and Maureen pack the boys into the car and head south to Calgary. It would be a full day starting with a free pancake breakfast, a trip to the midway, ending with the chuckwagon races before heading home.

They are seated on the first corner of the track in the Grandstand. It is the second-last race of the day. The canopy of each wagon advertises its sponsor—a car company, a telephone company, and of course, beer. The announcer's machine-gun-like voice, rat-tatted-tatted the race—*It's Smith in the Ford wagon with the lead as Felkirk in Casino by the River right beside followed on the outside by Mackenzie*—as the wagons round the final turn. The crowd yells and screams. The lead driver, wearing a black cowboy hat and mustard-yellow shirt, leans forward, knees pressing into the buckboard, hands whipping the reins, yee-hawing and giddy-upping his charges toward the twenty-five-thousand-dollar first prize when the inside wagon clips the guardrail, tips onto two wheels and somersaults the rider into the air. The wagon careens into the lead, causing a chain reaction. As the second driver is thrown from his wagon, the lead horse goes down. Reined together, the three other horses in the team plough into the track as the wagon rockets into the air, then crashes down into an explosion of wood and steel, bone and muscle. Horses whine and snort and neigh, their piercing cries a fatal and agonizing cacophony. Outriders jump off their horses, rush to the aid of the drivers while grounds workers spring into damage control, pulling large white tarps over the scene.

People stare horrified, mouths agape. Women and children cry. Men look at their boots. Families head toward the exits in waves, clutching children, midway toys, and prizes. The announcer attempts to assuage the growing panic and shock—and revulsion—over what has just unfolded before twenty thousand people. Maureen pulls Kenny and Patrick protectively into her, stifling their tears. Henry shakes his head. Mutters *Je-sus Christ* under his breath. Dale gapes at the crash, hands over his ears.

"What the fuck," Dale says. "What the fuck?"

Henry rises. "Let's go."

Maureen gives Henry a look as she squeezes Patrick's hand and begins to shuffle him and Kenny toward the stairs. Henry follows them up the grandstand and into the tunnel while he wraps his arm around Dale's shoulders and pulls him in close.

# DISNEYLAND

Maureen sits at the wooden picnic table in the lunchroom at Safeway, one eye on the tattered Disneyland guidebook, the other on Tom sitting beside her. He had given her the book two years ago. The table is painted the same green as a city park bench. Years of bums sliding on and off the seats, of food and drinks spilled and wiped up with chemical cleaners, has taken the sheen off the paint, making it look old and worn. Across from the table are two stacked rows of identical grey lockers staff are only allowed to use during their shift. They are not meant to store things they may want to hide from management, family, or the police. Maureen's white polyester uniform crinkles every time she moves. That she's overweight makes it that much worse. She sometimes sits in the lunchroom and thinks that her dream to take her husband, Henry, and three boys to Disneyland might actually become a reality.

"They'll love Pirates of the Caribbean. And Country Bear Jamboree. It's a bit hokey, but what the hell." Tom snaps his fingers, gives his shoulder a quick jig and begins to sing. "Look for the bare necessities, the simple bare necessities…"

She responds with a friendly elbow to his ribs.

"Stop it," she says with a laugh.

"What? It's from *The Jungle Book.*"

"Tom…"

"Just make sure you have as good a time as the boys. This will be as much your holiday as theirs. And don't forget to take the Monorail."

On Christmas Eve, Maureen frets late into the night. Before placing it under the tree, she wraps the guidebook and writes the boys' names on the rectangular label with reindeer pulling Santa in his sled. There are other gifts, of course, practical necessities like shirts, underwear, and socks. But this is *the* gift. It will make all three of her sons and maybe even Henry, who doesn't know of the surprise, jump up and down with joy. She has scrimped and saved over the past year, has even taken on extra shifts when she can, but is still unsure whether she will have enough money for the trip. Tom's reassured her. Said he will make sure she gets all the extra hours she will need in the New Year. Still, she worries. Maureen has put a deposit on the flights and is nervous about flying. Los Angeles airport is supposed to be ginormous. Tom's told Maureen that there are no grocery stores around Disneyland and you are not allowed to bring food inside. What if one of them gets lost? Robbed? Maureen has followed Tom's advice and has had the travel agent reserve a single room at a hotel directly across from the main entrance. It is more expensive but saves them having to rent a car. The two older boys, Dale and Patrick, will take sleeping bags and sleep on the floor. Kenny will sleep in a cot. Maureen and Henry will each get a single bed. They will all have to put up with Henry's snoring. The upside of squeezing everyone into one room will be the extra money the boys will have for souvenirs and the gifts Maureen will be able to bring back to send to her sisters.

It is not yet seven o'clock on Christmas morning when she is awoken by the muffled giggles and shushes to be quiet coming from the living room below. As she and Henry make their way downstairs, they listen to the shuffling of feet. Turning into the living room, they find Dale, Kenny, and Patrick sitting on the couch with little boy guilty-as-sin looks on their faces as they stare at the gift-wrapped packages under the tree.

The boys start with the boring stuff first, the clothing, candy. Then they give their mother gifts from school: Dale, a recipe holder made of painted Plexiglas; a tissue box Kenny's crafted out of Popsicle sticks; an abstract painting Patrick made in art class. The brothers grin in unison as Dale hands Henry his gift.

Besides drinking, Henry's only other joy is watching sports on television. During dark winter nights, he sits perched on the edge of his head-of-household chair, staring at the screen as men soldier up and down the ice, carving each other up with sticks, fists, and elbows. The more violent the game becomes, the more blood spills, the more belligerent Henry becomes. The boys watch solemnly as Henry transforms into the rabid fan popularized by beer commercials, rising to his feet, his fervour laced with profanities while he pounds his fists into the air.

When he unwraps the shoebox and looks inside, his hands begin to shake as he pulls out an Edmonton Oilers baseball cap and a single ticket to an Oilers versus the Leafs game. It does not matter that it is in the nosebleed section. He is going to an NHL game live featuring Grant Fuhr, Mark Messier, Jari Kurri, and the God of hockey—Wayne Gretzky. It is as if he has died and gone to heaven. Maureen smiles a knowing smile, having subsidized the boys' efforts to ensure their gift idea became a reality.

The brothers line up in front of the tree. The night before, Rock Paper Scissors determined who would be the gift giver. Beaming, Patrick and Dale bookend seven-year-old Kenny as he unfolds his hands to reveal a palm-sized, gift-wrapped jewellery box.

Maureen's heart leaps into her throat as she sits on the edge of the couch and slowly—too slowly for the boys—unwraps it. She removes the swath of cotton batting and gasps at the silver necklace with a dolphin pendant. She lifts it from the box and holds it against the back of her hand.

"Boys," she says, swallowing the strength of her feelings.

"We put all our money together," Kenny squeals. "You know, from raking leaves and picking pop bottle and cans."

"Awww," says Henry. "That's nice."

"I paid the most," Dale boasts.

"It don't matter who paid what," she says. Years after their mother died, Dale would confess that with the help of

Lance Mueller, he had shoplifted the necklace from Woodward's department store and had used the money they had saved to buy their father's hockey ticket.

"Come here," she whispers, wiping a tear from the corner of her eye with her free hand. She pulls the boys into her and kisses each of them on the cheek. "That's so nice."

"Put it on."

"Yeah, put it on."

Maureen threads the ends of the necklace around her neck and clicks the clasp together, the dolphin dangling against her housecoat. "I'll be wearing this until the day I die," she promises, looking at the boys one at a time. "Now," she says, rising to her feet, suddenly businesslike. She reaches her hand into the tree to pull out a small parcel envelope and hands it to Patrick.

"Patrick, you can have the honours."

"Mom," Dale complains.

"Shush," Henry warns.

"Careful…"

Patrick carefully rips open one edge of the envelope while Dale and Kenny hover over him. At first, they do not know what to make of this worn and dog-eared guidebook. Then it hits them.

"You're going to Disneyland," Henry cries out excitedly.

"The Happiest Place on Earth," Maureen adds. "The Happiest Place on Earth."

Two nights later, as the temperature plunged to -40 Celsius, Henry takes a taxi to the game, the baseball cap snug over his tuque. He is so worked up from the game that afterwards he ends up buying a round of drinks for strangers at the Dead Horse Tavern. At two in the morning, a taxi driver demanding a fare wakes Maureen up. She leads her drunk but happy husband upstairs, the tuque stuffed in his pocket, the baseball cap tipped back on his head. The cap will sit on his dresser collecting dust until years later when he is moved into a home, where he will die of Alzheimer's.

They never make it to Disneyland.

=

The light was fading when Kenny was pulled from the river. A voice on the phone informed Maureen that he had been found. Early in the spring, when the ice was deceptively thin and the river full, Kenny had fallen through and was swept away.

Henry said that identifying the dead was a man's job. Maureen would hear nothing of it. With grim determination, she accompanied him to the morgue. Years later, after he had a few drinks and thought that Patrick was old enough, he told him how fish, like birds of prey, go for the eyes first. He told him how his mother stood over Kenny's wrinkled body, bruised and battered from the rocky river bottom; how she ran a finger over his left forearm, elbow, and shoulder ; how she clutched the curled fingers of his right hand; and how, without a word, she wept, bending down to kiss his fish-charred lips. She closed her eyes, smiled, and whispered in his ear.

Henry did not shed a tear at Kenny's funeral, his stoicism a reflection of his view of death being a life lesson. Patrick knew why his father did not cry. He could not cry.

Dale was with Kenny when he drowned. Henry had yelled at Kenny after he burnt the toast. It was more than an argument. It was, as it had been for the longest time, Henry against the world. So, Dale took Kenny with him to the fort by the river. Sitting on a log while Kenny explored the bank, Dale turned his head while trying to light a small camp stove the brothers kept hidden. It was a moment that would torment him for the rest of his life. He did not see or stop Kenny from crawling out on a tree branch that extended over the water where he suffered an asthma attack. Clutching his throat, Kenny lost his balance, toppled through the ice and into the water.

Not surprisingly, Henry laid the blame squarely on Dale's shoulders. "What do you mean, you turned your back?" he snarled, days after. For him it was black and white. Dale was the oldest. It was his job—his job—to protect his younger brother. Yet the truth was, their father was woefully inadequate at protecting anyone but himself.

Patrick did not get to see Kenny's body. Something about him being in the water too long. During the funeral, he clutched his mother's damp hand. Or rather, she clung to his, sobbing inconsolably, her hands shaking, never letting his go. A few weeks after the service, Maureen and Henry came home with a green aluminum urn. She promptly placed it on the kitchen counter beside the chipped, black-and-white cow cookie jar. "If Kenny wants a chocolate chip cookie, it'll be right there beside him," she quipped, giving the urn a pat with her hand. Within days, a shrine bloomed around it—baby pictures, school photos, bits of wood and pebbles that Kenny had collected. It was weird to reach for a cookie with the remains of your brother in the way. Patrick always thought, what if? Luckily, the goose neck opening of the urn prevented anyone from reaching in for a cookie and accidentally coming up with a handful of dust. The longer it remained in the kitchen, the more it became a source of embarrassment and derision: the uncomfortable snickers and sideway glances from family and friends, the neighbours' whispered gossip suggested that people were beginning to question Maureen's sanity. Yes, you do not lose a son without going off the deep end, if only a bit.

On the first anniversary of Kenny's death, Maureen took a piece of toast and whipped it across the room at Henry.

"If you hadn't thrown the toast at him, he'd be alive today," she screamed.

Henry threw the toast because he had to. If he wasn't throwing toast, or shoes, or jackets, or cursing and swearing at someone, he was doing whatever he could to maintain his fleeing control over his family. Bravado, chest thumping, and threats aside, Henry knew his grasp was waning. Dale was beginning to tower over him. Patrick would soon follow.

Maureen continued to take her anger out on Henry. She hit him. Slapped him. Insulted him. Had nothing to do with him in the bedroom. Yet, this man of sinew and muscle took the hectoring and histrionics with the meek acceptance of a defeated man. It was, it seemed, poetic justice.

Maureen began taking on as many extra shifts at work as she could. Henry knew it was good for her. She came home from work in high spirits talking incessantly about Tom. Tom this. Tom that.

"What the hell is it with you and Tomato Tom?" he charged one morning while Maureen was packing her lunch for work.

"Don't call him names."

"I'll call him whatever I like."

"We're friends, that's all," Maureen said, grabbing her lunch bag off the kitchen counter. "Don't forget the vacuuming,"

And walked out the door.

It was when Maureen started to come home with extra produce, slightly damaged fruit and vegetables, good enough to eat but not good enough to be sold, that Henry's suspicions began to grow. He took to accompanying Maureen to the grocery story and would follow obediently behind, pushing the cart, always on the alert, looking for a sign, whenever they were in the produce section. It was as he was putting mushrooms into a paper bag one day and Tom leaned over and said hello that it all made sense. The fragrance of Tom's aftershave wafted into the air—the same fragrance he had detected on Maureen's clothing just days before. As Tom turned away, Henry knew he had no choice but to turn a blind eye to whatever irrational pleasure his wife found with this cipher of a man who filled display bins with fruit and vegetables for a living. It was as if it were well-deserved punishment for throwing toast at their son. Henry remained stoic, faithful, believing, as he told Patrick years later, that if this was Maureen's way of coping, so be it.

Things only got worse the day Henry announced he'd accepted a position to become a foreman at the plant. His decision further fuelled Maureen's hostility. There were to be no white shirts in this house, she raged. Dale cursed him and stormed out the door. She threatened to kick Henry out when he started to argue that they needed the money and that he took the job for the family. She could spend the extra money however she wished. She wanted nothing to do with his dirty money. Out of spite, anger, or both, instead Henry bought a used Buick Electra at auction. Maureen fumed.

The next summer, Maureen abruptly stood during dinner.

"It's time to put Kenny to rest." She walked across the room, pulled the urn off the counter, and headed toward the front door.

"Where're you going?" asked Henry.

"Where do you think?"

"I'm not going," Dale said.

"You don't have to. You've suffered enough," she acknowledged, casting a dark glance in Henry's direction.

Henry and Patrick followed Maureen into the river valley. By now, she waddled more than she walked and wore her weight with pride. As they made their way to the tree that Kenny fell from, joggers and dogwalkers gave her, a large woman wearing a fraying sweater, torn jeans, and slippers, and clutching a green aluminum urn, a wide berth.

Clouds scudded across the sky as the river valley funnelled a cool breeze from the north. A gull swooped down, swooshed overhead, before winging toward the opposing shore. Maureen stepped calf-deep into the water. She turned and faced the eastern sun. Stroked the urn. With two hands she held the urn high above her head. With a flick of her wrists, a stream of pancake-looking powder poured out and scattered across the surface of the water. White flecks of her middle son floated on top of the water before being pulled under, just as he had been. She turned, her legs red from the freezing water, and stared at Henry, his arms limp at his side.

"I..." he began. He turned away.

Maureen opened her mouth as if to speak. She turned back to the river, leaned on her right foot and tossed the urn, football-like, as far into the river as she could. It bobbed and weaved with the current before sinking. As she stepped back to shore, she slipped and fell, the water up to her knees, and wept.

"I just want to see him one last time," she pleaded.

Patrick was too afraid to tell his mother that he had seen Kenny. Months ago, as the winter sky darkened, Patrick had wanted to be alone. He made his way to the fort, careful to avoid damaging the cross-country trails as he trudged down the valley. He paused to gaze wide-eyed at the northern lights that bleached the black sky. When he reached the fort, Patrick lay on his back and continued to stare at the avalanche of light, scarves of blue, green, and turquoise quivering and crackling. He pulled out a mickey of whiskey he'd snitched from the house. The first drop numbed his bottom lip and spread a tingle through his mouth. Next, a quick series of sips; each burned his throat. Each was a good burn. An adult burn. Dizzy, he chipped an icicle off a nearby branch, broke it into small pieces and watched, mesmerized, as the pieces mixed with the rye. From sip to swig, he drank. Gagged. His head froze as his stomach burned. As Patrick arched his head to the sky, he stumbled and fell face first into the snow. He pushed himself up with his hands and knees onto a log. He closed his eyes. Sensed the liquor curling through his chest and lungs, warming him while his stomach churned. When he exhaled, he closed his eyes, sensing the liquor as it regurgitated as one thick burp that momentarily lodged in his throat before flaring his nostrils red. When Patrick opened his eyes, he saw Kenny, dense as he was light, standing translucent on the river past where he had fallen through. He was smiling, his eyes aglow. As he lifted his arm and stretched his index finger toward the northern lights, the night sky burst with light, wrenching Patrick's sense of loss while pulling Kenny to the north and beyond.

Patrick was awoken with the jolt of someone shaking his shoulders.

Dale towered over him his eyes wide with fear.

"You can't do this," Dale said as he pulled Patrick into him, wrapped his arms around him, the heat from his body transferring to his brother's. "You can't pull a Kenny on me."

# THE RABBIT

When the days stretched long into summer, Henry, tired of the kill, would entice his son Patrick to go for a Sunday ride with him with the promise of ice cream. Rising from the couch, pulling a worn baseball cap from the closet, he would signal his intentions by rattling the set of keys that dangled from his hand. "Coming?" he would say, flipping the cap onto his head and heading out the door. It was an order. Not an offer.

Their first stop was always the local gas bar. It was just a few blocks from the small, rented house they lived in. The station was nothing more than a shack that, as well as selling gasoline, oil, and windshield washer fluid, offered up lottery tickets, withered hot dogs, stale donuts, chocolate bars, and soft drinks. The men's washroom dispensed colognes from one coin-operated machine, condoms from another. Two quarters got you a squirt of a choice of three colognes while a dollar gave buyers the option of rainbow-coloured or ribbed condoms. Most important, the gas bar had a Slurpee machine and an ice-cream freezer. While Patrick peered into the freezer, deciding on the treat of the day, his father would order a large cola Slurpee and disappear into the bathroom. "Gotta have a whiz," he would say with a wink and a shrug of his shoulder, the Slurpee container firmly in his hand.

It was the time that his father grinned and pulled open his jean jacket just enough to show off the silver flask in the inside pocket that Patrick understood why his mother was so visibly upset every time Henry insisted Patrick accompany him on his Sunday drive. Once behind the bathroom door, Henry would pour out just enough Slurpee to accommodate the rye whiskey in the flask. He would come out of the bathroom with a big grin on his face, grab a pack of gum or Tic Tac mints off the shelf before heading out the door. Sometimes, he would buy a lottery ticket with whatever change remained. "What the heck," he would joke, telling Patrick that if he ever won, he would buy a farm, work it for a few years, go broke, and then return to his job at the meat processing plant.

Leaving the city, they would head north and east with no particular destination in mind. Henry's view of the world was that a man didn't work unless he used his back. To emphasize his point, he would gaze at the plume of smoke coming from distant red and white towers. "You know what that is?" he would ask, breathing in deeply while pointing a nicotine-stained finger in the direction of refinery row. "The smell of money. Union guys in there pull in twelve, fourteen dollars an hour. And they're just the Joe Blows like me. Tradesmen, pipefitters, electricians, millwrights...who knows what they make. Throw in some overtime, and you're sitting pretty, driving a new truck every three years. All you got to do is get your journeyman's ticket, do what you're told to do and you end up with a half decent living. Not bad, I would say."

Patrick couldn't fathom how someone who shot bolts into the heads of bawling cows for a living could tell him what he should be doing with his life. Besides, Patrick already knew where he was headed. He was going to be famous. He was going to be on the radio. Patrick would be the next Eddie Spam, the morning man on the radio station, CJOD. Patrick woke up every morning to Eddie Spam's booming voice, silly jokes. He sometimes saw him in person, at the summer fair, standing outside car dealerships waving to passing drivers, or inside malls at Christmas. Everything about Eddie Spam was big—the ten-gallon cowboy hat he wore out in public; his whiter than white porcelain teeth that clacked when he spoke; the intensely bright blue eyes matched only by his rhinestone-studded, baby-blue suit that covered his broad-shouldered six-foot-plus frame. His voice, both on and off air, boomed. Patrick was determined to be the next Eddie Spam. He would go to college, get his start in a small hick town where he would get the girls and the big car that Milton Schmidt bragged that his cousin who worked at a radio station in Brandon, Manitoba got. All he had to do was talk, make people laugh. Be friendly. It all sounded so easy.

Thus, it was the radio, not his father's words, that kept Patrick's attention as they drove the backwoods of Alberta. He would pass the time listening to the voices coming out of the speakers, silently mimicking the enthusiasm the afternoon jockey had for a one-hit country artist hit or the sombre inflections of the top-of-the-hour news announcer. Oblivious of his son's feigned attention, Henry would take long draws from his straw and stare off into the distance as a film of sweat on the outside of the container slowly spread to his crotch. His right hand firmly on the steering wheel, Henry would twiddle a lit cigarette between his fingers. His left forearm, with its deep blue veins pressing against the tanned skin, muscles taut from killing, rested on the window panel, elbow to the wind. Even on cool days, he would insist on leaving open a small crack in the driver's side window. Having heard that cigarettes affected the vocal chords, Patrick would plug his nose and take in small breaths, watching out of the corner of his eye as a contrail of smoke was sucked out his father's window. Before long, the combination of booze and tobacco would fill the car with a pungent smell. When it became too much to bear, Patrick would open his window and turn his head to breathe in the country air.

=

Henry was taking a deep draw on his straw when he glanced into the rear-view mirror. The look of alarm on his father's face forced Patrick to look into the passenger side mirror, along the sleek lines of his father's Buick Electra. An RCMP cruiser trailed them, its red and blue lights flashing. As Henry turned the car onto the shoulder, he cursed, pulled it to a stop, popped a couple of Tic Tacs into his mouth, and handed Patrick the Slurpee container. "Don't spill it," Henry ordered with a wink.

Henry had just swallowed the last of the breath mints when the constable, a young woman with strawberry blonde hair tucked up under her cap, approached them. She angled herself behind the driver's door and assessed the situation, suspicious of someone driving an expensive car that was clearly beyond the driver's means. It seemed apparent from the way she looked at Henry that the constable thought he was either an eccentric millionaire with a young boy in the passenger seat or a petty criminal who had purchased the car through ill-gotten means. They exchanged the usual pleasantries. She asked for his licence and registration. The woman kept her eyes on Patrick while Henry reached into the glove box, assessing his safety. Her only response when Henry asked, in a curt voice, what he had done wrong, was to demand that they both stay in the car. She then returned to her cruiser, licence and registration in hand. Henry's eyes narrowed. He called her a bitch under his breath. He flexed his jaw. Stiffened his arms. Wrapped his fingers around the steering wheel. As he shifted his gaze between the rear-view mirror and the side-view mirror, Henry flipped the Tic Tac container open with his thumb, emptied a couple of mints into the palm of his hand, and slipped them into his mouth. Henry then shoved the candy container between the crack in the front seat and sat still. The Slurpee cup, now tucked between Patrick's legs, numbed his groin. The red plastic straw, wet with a sliver of Henry's saliva, protruded from the container lid.

The crunch of the constable's boots against the gravel signalled her return. As she leaned into the car to return the papers to Henry, the yellow piping of her RCMP issued trousers bent with her knees. She peered across the seat at Patrick. Fearful, he grabbed the container and sucked deep into the straw. The combination of cola and whiskey hit the back of his mouth like fire and ice. He choked and gagged. A stream of brown liquid dripped from his nose. He swallowed back the urge to throw up before putting his hand to his forehead, dizzy from the rush of the liquor.

"You okay?" she asked, her voice friendly.

"Ice-cream headache," Patrick stuttered, pinching his nose with his thumb and finger while keeping a firm grip on the container, lest he spill it and expose his father's offence.

She smiled understandingly.

"Drive carefully now," she said to Henry as she handed him his registration and walked away.

Henry sat with his hands on his lap, silently staring at the cruiser as it disappeared down the road. He looked at his son with a smile. "Dodged that bullet now, didn't we?" His father, reaching over to return the registration to the glove compartment with his left hand while jabbing Patrick in the ribs with his right middle index finger. "You little shit," he continued, his voice proud as he leaned back into his seat and held out his hand, demanding his drink back.

They continued. It was a hot, cloudless day. The urban sprawl had long surrendered to farmland with its rolling hills and ravines lined with copses of lodgepole and jack pine, poplar and willow trees, flat farmers' fields brimful of spring wheat, barley, and alfalfa. Abandoned sheds, their wood exteriors grey with age, stood canted from the wind. A fox sat still on a rise and sniffed the air. Black and white magpies and other scavenger birds ragged across the clear blue sky or sat patiently on fence posts along the side of the road waiting for cars and trucks to provide them with their next meal.

Patrick had gotten used to his father's silence. There were times he thought his father didn't even know he was in the seat beside him. Driving seemed to be a refuge, a source of solitude for Henry. There was a particular sense of contentment that would come over him as he drove the open spaces, the wind blowing through the windows, the cloudless blue sky stretching as far as the eye could see. Sometimes Henry would break into a quiet hum. Other times he would say a few words or point to wildlife. During one ride, Henry pointed to a couple of magpies and told Patrick about that story he'd read in the newspaper about refugees who were caught with a burlap bag full of them. They were planning to fry them up for dinner. "Stupid slant eyes," Henry said with a chuckle as he sucked on his cigarette. Patrick cringed, appalled at the thought of the surely awful-tasting, meagre meal that would come from such a dumb bird. Then there was the time Henry told Patrick that when he was behind the wheel of the Electra he was beholden to nobody but himself. Driving gave him the chance to get away from it all, the fighting, the bickering, just as Patrick and his older Dale would disappear into their fort down in the valley near the edge of the North Saskatchewan River for the same reason. Or rather used to. After seeing Kenny fall through the ice and drown two winters ago, Dale no longer ventured down into the valley.

When they passed the occasional farmer on his tractor or combine, Henry would offer up a friendly wave. The operator would often respond with a small gesture, a nod, knowing that no farmer in his right mind would be caught driving a gas guzzler like a Buick Electra. Often, after hitting a larger than usual pothole, Henry would pat the dashboard with his fingers, as if to reassure the car that it would be all right. There, there, he would say. Or Sorry. It was one of the few times Patrick remembered his father saying that word. Sorry.

As they travelled a dirt concession road in a trail of dust, Henry approached a steep hill leading to a small bridge that crossed a small stream. Patrick gazed up at a hawk soaring in an arching circle high in the sky. Henry had just pulled the Electra into a blind curve at the bottom of the hill when he cursed and jammed on the brakes. The car slid on the oil-slicked gravel road and skidded to a stop. Henry looked at his crotch. While stopping, he had squeezed the Slurpee container with his thighs, spilling the contents onto his jeans. He glared at Patrick, handed him the container, smiled as he licked his right fingers with a single flick of his tongue, rubbed the remains of the sugary liquid into his denim jeans and gazed out the windshield at the woman.

=

In a neighbourhood where houses corresponded like worn pieces of a Monopoly game, where used pickup trucks and rust-bucket subcompact cars were the norm, a weather-beaten lipstick-red Buick Electra stood out. Rock chips sprayed the paint. The windshield had the obligatory prairie bolt-of-lightning crack across the glass. Henry refused to replace it, arguing that the moment he got the windshield fixed would be the moment a passing truck would spit out a rock and break it all up again. Pasted onto the rear was a bumper sticker. It read, "Please Lord, send another oil boom. We promise we won't piss it away next time." Henry was informed that the previous owner, who had gone bankrupt speculating on oil leases, had slapped the sticker on just as the bailiffs were coming up the driveway to repossess it. A set of purple fuzzy dice hung from the rear-view mirror— homage to the rebel spirit of the woman.

Starting the 350 horsepower, 4-barrel carburetor engine was like shoving money in one end and blowing it out the other. When the car lumbered down the street, neighbours cast looks that varied from consternation to envy. The driver was either a drug dealer or a country-twang gigolo looking for some action. Naturally, whenever Henry lifted the hood to check the oil or change the air filter, some neighbour looky-loo, more often than not with a beer in his hand, would amble over to offer some friendly advice.

Maureen screamed bloody murder when Henry pulled this boat of a car to the curb in front of the house. The childish grin on his face only made things worse. There she was sitting at the kitchen table clipping grocery coupons and comparing flyers while Henry was at an auto auction bidding on a car with triple digits on the odometer and upholstery that smelled of stale perfume, bath salts and liquor. Maureen refused to even sit in the car, never mind drive it. It wasn't so much that she didn't want to drive the car. She was afraid of it. What if she had to, God forbid, parallel park? Either way, it didn't matter. The car was Henry's pride and joy. Anyone could see by the look on his face when he slid into the driver's seat and paused before turning the key that this car was more than a mere mode of transportation. It was his one treat in life, his escape, if only temporary, from the curse of the working-class. As a compromise, Henry agreed to chauffeur Maureen around on her Saturday shopping expedition. He would park the car as close to the entrance as possible and sit in the front seat listening to country radio while Maureen walked up and down the aisles at the neighbourhood Safeway store or shopped for bargains at the Army and Navy department store.

=

A baby-blue Ford Escort, its engine off, was stopped in the middle of the road. A young woman, dressed in tight-fitting jeans and a loose-fitting T-shirt, stood near the front, bent forward, staring at something on the ground in front of the car. She was blonde. Her hair fell forward towards her breasts. She straightened at the waist, pulling the shirt taunt, revealing that she was not wearing a bra. Upon seeing her small stone-sized nipples pressing against the white cotton, Patrick sensed a redness growing in his cheeks. The woman's shoulder sagged. She dropped her hands to her side and stared mournfully at the Electra. Henry studied her for just a moment. He pushed his hair from his forehead with his right hand, put the car into park and pushed down the emergency brake with his foot as the woman walked toward them.

"Stay in the car," he ordered, handing Patrick the container.

Henry skimmed his fingers across his damp crotch and sniffed the palm of his hand before pulling on the door latch. As he stepped from the car, Henry glanced both ways for approaching traffic. They met in front of the Electra. The woman thanked Henry profusely. Afraid she would see him staring at her nipples, which seemed to continue to grow, Patrick slouched into his seat. Seeing him, the woman offered a tight, nervous smile before lowering her voice, whispering in a protective tone that made Patrick feel as if they were talking about him, as if he had done something wrong. Patrick watched as his father took in the woman's words with a respectful silence. They walked to the front of the Escort. He stared as she gestured to the ground. A grim look crossed his face.

"It just jumped out," the woman said. "There was nothing I could do."

"It's probably best you put it out of its misery," Patrick overheard his father say.

As the Electra engine thrummed in his ears, Patrick eased open the passenger door, dropped to his knees, crept along the side of the front panel, peered past the front tire, and snuck a look. A rabbit lay inert on its right side in front of the Escort, its coal-black eyes bulging with fear. It stared at Patrick. Its nose quivered. The rabbit's ears occasionally twitched. It looked no more in pain than the pets at school. Then Patrick saw the rabbit's rump. The tail was crushed flat into the dirt. Its hind legs were broken, one bent towards the sky. Brown and white fur was peppered with bits of blood. The rabbit kneaded its front claws into the road forming small divots in the dirt.

Except the occasional bird breaking its neck by flying into the living room window, Patrick had never seen something dying right before his eyes. A bird was one thing. But this, this, was a *rabbit,* a real-life Bugs Bunny, something sweet and soft and furry that you were supposed to take home with you.

The ground around them was splashed with rays of the sun coming through the trees. The only sound, other than the car engine, was the nattering of a couple of magpies waiting in the wings. The woman drew her fingers nervously across her lips. She closed her eyes, clearly at wits' end. Her hand shook as she patted her brow with the back of her hand. As she opened her eyes, she saw Patrick crouched alongside the car. It was as if he was intruding on something illicit between his father and the woman. Henry's eyes followed hers. Father and son froze. His father's glare confirmed that Patrick had entered a world he had no business being in. Then, as Henry took a step towards Patrick, the rabbit emitted the most awful sound Patrick had ever heard. It was a low, ear-piercing peep. Patrick dropped to his knees and stared at the O the rabbit had formed with its mouth. He watched in disbelief, swallowing back tears as the rabbit frantically dug its front claws into the ground as this plaintive whine that pierced the  woods, refracted off the leaves, bounced off the trees, this agonizing note that rang across the countryside forever and ever, this pleading to anyone and anything, that the rabbit was hurt, in pain, and yes, dying, but above all there was nothing, nothing, anyone could do or anything that could be done. It was at that moment, as his father stared at him, that Patrick saw for the first time, this man who killed for a living, a cold and casual indifference towards death with the injured rabbit and this distraught woman being nothing more than an interruption to his Sunday drive. Behind that cold, angry glare was someone who had lost the ability to give life. What Patrick saw that Sunday in his father, he witnessed again three years later when his mother died. The death of a supposed loved one was nothing more than an inconvenience.

The peeping stopped. The woman moaned, choking back tears.

Patrick sensed that his father had been resigned to putting the rabbit out of its misery the moment she told him what had happened. Henry stared at the woman. He shook his head, curled his lower lip.

"Go with..." he began, looking at the lady.

"Melinda," she stammered.

"Go with Melinda," he ordered, turning to his son. "I'll be there in a few minutes."

It was not the time to argue. Patrick followed Melinda to her car.

"Wait at the top of the hill."

Melinda bit her lower lip and watched as Patrick climbed into the passenger seat. She started up the Escort, reversed it around the Electra, careful not to hit the rabbit, before pulling a three-point turn and turning up the hill in the direction Henry and Patrick had come. As they passed, Patrick gazed at his father. He had pulled another cigarette from the pack and was smoking, staring down at the rabbit. Through the side-view mirror, Patrick watched Henry let the cigarette drop out of his hand and stub it out with his foot before turning to the Electra. He was not one to waste a smoke.

"Poor thing just jumped out of the bush," Melinda explained as she drove up the hill. "There was nothing I could do."

As she parked the car and turned off the motor, Patrick listened for the rumble of the Electra engine.

"It's a man's work, isn't it?" she said.

"What is?"

"Killing." Her eyes were full of fear..

"I guess so."

Patrick knew it would be quick. Clean. The revving of the Electra's engine confirmed that the car was moving towards its intended target. Patrick reached over and grabbed the radio knob.

The woman gripped his hand, uncertain as to what he was about to do. She stared into his eyes and released her grip. "Sorry."

Patrick turned the radio on low and stared out the window, tuning in with one ear to the latest hit from the tinny-sounding A.M. station while listening to the Electra with the other. As he stared out across the farmer's field, at the ripe, golden, waist-high grain wavering in the summer breeze, he cringed, and closed his eyes, imagined his father, his face sombre, hunched over the steering wheel, country tunes rattling from the Electra's worn-out speakers as he lined the driver's side tire with the rabbit. He saw the long face of the doomed rabbit, its eyes black with fear, its nose and ears twitching uncontrollably, its claws ripped red as it frantically dug into the oily road as if it could somehow miraculously bury itself below ground level safe from death, yet unable to do anything but stare and claw, claw and stare, as a ton of red steel and chrome crept toward it.

The shifting of gears signalled that Henry was turning the car around, a confirmation that he had completed what the woman had asked him to do.

"Your dad. Is he a farmer?"

"With a car like that? Not likely."

"What does he do? For a living?"

The engine returned to a steady idle. The time between the sound of the car door opening and closing told Patrick that his father had disposed of the rabbit in the ditch. The magpies let out a collective warble of delight.

"He works at the Tanner meatpacking plant."

The woman cringed.

"He kills the livestock as they come in," Patrick continued with a feigned sense of pride. "With a bolt gun." Patrick began to make a trigger with his thumb and forefinger. The woman put up her hand. She shook her head and turned away.

He's good at it."

"Good at?" she asked.

"Killing things."

Patrick turned off the radio, climbed out of the car and awaited his father's return.

# ROOM 302 OF THE BLUE BUFFALO MOTEL

Maureen sits on the edge of an unmade bed in room 302 of the Blue Buffalo Motel. It is the room where she and Tom Nicholson, the produce manager at the Safeway where she works, always meet, whenever they can, often on a Tuesday afternoon. She cannot fathom calling him her lover, nor even make herself say that word. It sounds so foreign. Neither can she bear to think they may just be—well—*fucking*. The word reminds her of being fresh out of high school and alone in the city. She would get drunk at a bar and wake up the next morning in bed with someone whose name she could not remember or cared to know.

As he prepares to head home, Maureen watches Tom preen in front of the cracked bathroom mirror. She knows that he lives on the respectable side of the river, home to good schools and indoor shopping malls. He has two teenaged stepdaughters, a boy who excels at hockey, and a bottled-blonde wife called Kate who sells real estate when she's not doing whatever it is that suburban wives do with their time. Maureen has met Kate at the annual staff Christmas parties and summer barbeques. She is prim and pretty, a snotty woman with her nose stuck in the air and a Barbie-doll-fake-n-bake tan. What Maureen notices most about Kate is how each year her wrinkles look that much longer, that much deeper.

Maureen has never thought of Tom as particularly good-looking, although at times she sees hints of a youthful handsomeness he's now lost to middle age. His teeth are crooked and yellowed, and what little hair he has left he keeps unfashionably long on the sides. She's often seen him use his bowling-ball paunch to prop up fruit and vegetables he's piling onto the display counters. When they're together, he no longer looks at her, nor does he undress her like he did when they first started meeting in room 302. Maureen wonders if she's become no more than that to him now—produce to be consumed and dispensed with.

"This has to end," she says, slipping frayed bra straps over her rounded shoulders, reaching for the blouse she dropped on the floor when they arrived. A smirk crosses his face. He pats down his hair and tucks in his shirt, his eyes a calculating hardness. "I'm serious," she continues, slipping the blouse over her head and allowing it to drape over the folds of flesh that muffin-top her jeans. "There's just too much going on with Henry and Dale. The strike."

"What's that got to do with us?"

"Nothing. Everything."

Henry is a foreman at Tanner's. Dale works on the production line. Henry got his son on at the meatpacking plant after he dropped out of school, thinking a few weeks around the blood and gore would be enough to convince him of the importance of an education. Then the owner, Tim Tanner, locked out the workers and brought in scab workers Henry must now supervise. The vitriol between father and son grows evermore every day, each bringing his differences, anger, and frustrations home. Just last night, Henry chased Dale out the front door, reminding him that he was lucky to have a roof over his head with the little strike pay he gets.

Maureen reaches for the necklace she placed on the bedside table. The necklace, with its dolphin pendant, was a present from her three sons. Since her middle son died, she's only taken it off when Tom and she are together—lest a loose finger or inadvertent thumb catch and break the chain. She sits on the unmade bed and waits for Tom to finish whatever it is he does in the bathroom. Stepping out, he taps his watch with his index finger. He always cites the need to beat the afternoon traffic when he's ready to go. Maureen too must get home. Henry's off work at four.

Their time together is predictable. Tom picks Maureen up at a bus stop a block from the motel. He registers at the front desk, always paying with cash, while she sits in his car, picking at her fingers, keeping warm and low in the front seat, eyes glued to 302's door with its faded golden plastic numbers, the door's pink paint chipped and time bleached. From the start, she's thought it odd that a one-storey motel would have numbers running in the two and three hundreds. Like their affair, maybe it helps give the motel a sense that there's more to it than meets the eye. Tom always struts from the motel office toward the car, his face looking giddy . When he returns the oversized key, he will turn and teasingly dangle it at her before going into the motel office.

Once inside the room, small talk is followed by silence as they undress and quickly climb into bed. Maureen always feels tempted to pull back the covers to check for bed bugs or a strand of pubic hair like she used to when she first arrived in the city and worked as a hotel housekeeper. She holds back, knowing it would take away from whatever the moment may possibly be.

Maureen has grown large over the years. She's made it clear she's not keen to try anything that might overstress her joints. Tom presses into her, moaning and groaning. The production of bodily fluids culminates with a long-winded sigh as he rolls onto his back to stare at the ceiling. Maureen was initially surprised to find trivial differences between being with him and being with Henry—Tom wears aftershave and Henry no longer does.

Maureen often thinks about the other women Tom has probably brought to the motel. No doubt he brought Susan Macluski. Susan is a single mother and lives three doors down from Maureen in a house she rents, which smells of rotting grass and dirty socks. Her kids look tired, and their clothes look like they were pulled right off the clothesline. When Maureen and Susan met, Susan worked as a waitress at the Riverside Golf Course during the summer and collected unemployment during the winter. When they'd had a drink or two—which was often— Susan would boast that the golf club gave her the chance to grab rich balls. One day Susan told Maureen the produce manager at the local Safeway store—after she'd chatted him up about Brussels sprouts and the size of carrots—suggested she apply as a cashier. Not long after, Susan confided that she and the produce manager were doing some planting of their own. Susan did not even make it past her probationary period before being fired for calling in sick once too often. The last time Maureen spoke to Susan, she was back waitressing at the club, trying to squeeze whatever balls she could.

"Can I touch it?" Tom asked her one day as he stared at the dolphin necklace while sitting with Maureen in the Safeway lunchroom.

You're a cheeky one, aren't you, Maureen thought, thinking of Susan.

"It's just a dolphin."

Tom paused, waiting for silent permission before pressing the ends of his fingers, ever so lightly, into her sternum as he lifted the pendant.

"Kate and the kids swam with dolphins during our last trip to Hawaii. I've got the pictures to prove it. You should go sometime."

Maureen smiled. Hawaii, like so many other things in her life, was nothing more than a fantasy.

"The boys gave it to me for Christmas," she replied with a mother's pride. It had been Dale, Kenny, and Patrick's response to listening to her sigh enviously as the temperature dropped outside and vacation commercials—couples lounging on white beaches, families frolicking in clear blue water—kept her eyes glued to the television. The boys had pooled their money together to buy her the necklace. It was the same year she and Henry had surprised the family with an announcement that they were going to Disneyland. Then Kenny died.

Tom had offered Maureen a consoling shoulder to cry on. When she was down, which was often, Tom would offer Maureen a comforting hug, a quiet coffee in the empty lunchroom, a pat on the shoulder, a reassuring, "You'll be all right." He gave her tips on managing customers while struggling with her grief. "When you work with the public, you have to at least appear to like people, even when you don't," he said. "It's not like you have to like-like them. You only have to pretend to like them." Over the years, Tom had gotten particularly good at hiding his contempt for the public behind a pasty smile, one usually only used by bored Hollywood actors and celebrities standing on the red carpet during awards season.

Soon he began to talk more personally with Maureen. Tom was a Safeway lifer. He had started stocking shelves part-time in high school, and then dropped out of college to work full-time. He told her that he could now spot an overripe cantaloupe from twenty feet away. He loathed having to deal with suppliers and staff, above all the uppity Safeway chain of command who trudged in from head office oozing testosterone. They would look around the store with probing eyes trying to find something amiss.

Late one shift, six months after Kenny's funeral, he snuck a quick kiss on her cheek in the back of the store. Maureen was not sure what to make of this, but it made her realize that she could not recall the last time Henry, as grief-stricken as he was, had kissed her. Maybe it was at a New Year's Eve party because that's what you do at the stroke of midnight. Kiss the one you love. Let bygones be bygones. Hope for the better.

When Tom first proposed they meet at the Blue Buffalo Motel, Maureen turned him down flat. To what end, she thought. An hour of what? Why not at least a Holiday Inn? Over the course of the next few months he winked, nudged, and cajoled her until he finally wore her down.

"I know what you're going through," Tom said after their third time in room 302. He'd been unusually quiet and in no hurry to leave. "It doesn't get any easier." He lay beside her in his undershorts, barely breathing. "Jamie was three," Tom continued, his voice low. Maureen felt the muscles in her stomach tighten. Never in a million years would she have guessed that Tom had lost a child. "He was born with a heart condition. We could do nothing but love him. There are better ways now. But that was then. His death broke up my marriage."

"Oh, Tom."

"What doesn't kill you makes you stronger," he replied with a dry laugh. "Death by a thousand tears is more like it." He ran his hands over his face. "Carol was my high-school sweetheart. Yes," he said, reacting to Maureen's sharp look. "People still marry their high-school sweethearts. I was a biology major, hoping to get into veterinary school. When it got to be too much I dropped out of school to work full time. Then Jamie died. Carol began visiting her sister in Calgary. Soon she was visiting her every weekend and ended up marrying an oil man ten years older than her. Now she's a stay-at-home mom with three kids in private school, a dog, and a condo in Hawaii." He looked at her, resigned. "As for me and Kate and the kids? She's got her real estate. I've got my... I don't know what I got." He winked. "Or gotten myself into."

Tom usually drives Maureen to the bus stop so she can return as she came. In winter, when a particularly bitter cold front settles onto the city and turns waiting in an unheated bus shelter into a form of cruel punishment, Tom sometimes drives her close to her home—near enough to get her home quickly, but far enough away from prying eyes.

Soon after they began seeing each other, Tom started giving Maureen bags of produce. "A token of my appreciation," he announced the first time he handed her a plastic Safeway bag full of peppers and carrots. The bags contained vegetables shoppers would not touch: perfectly edible, yet with small deformities—a double-legged carrot that somehow got missed at the packing plant or a slightly discoloured pepper—goods that could bruise the store's reputation if put on public display. It seemed to be a charitable gesture since produce trucked in from California and Mexico during the winter months was prohibitively expensive. At first, the gifts embarrassed Maureen. True, Henry did drive a cab part-time when the line at the plant went down for annual maintenance or during the holiday season. Kenny's funeral had drained them financially.

The produce changed something between them. Before long Maureen expected the bags, even though she found the exchange —fruits and vegetables for sex—unsettling. Not that she thought of herself as being like one of those scarecrows who stood shivering at truck stops or on street corners at all hours of the day. She cringed at the thought of the men who had sex with those women, with their scabies, STDs, and AIDS, before they went home to kiss their wives and kids good night. How desperate could a man be for something as simple as sex?

Tom started bringing other things—undies, a bra—the sexy sort of stuff that Henry would not even fathom buying Maureen. Like most women, Maureen knew the novelties were not for her. Tom admitted, with a sly grin, that knowing what lay behind the door to room 302 was a bit of a turn-on.

What Tom really did for her—what nobody else could do—was to make her laugh, like the time he surprised her with a novelty bra that had been marked down after Christmas at a sex specialty store. Red with bells, it jingled so much during sex that the two of them broke into laughter so hard they could not finish what they had started.

At times, sex with Tom was no different than changing the laundry. He would sometimes insist on taking her from behind. Maureen would get on her knees, hands gripping the top edge of the mattress, face down in a thin pillow that reeked of the previous guests, bed squeaking and squealing as Tom sweated, grunted, and bucked like the middle-aged man with a bad back that he was, all the while grinning—she knew without being able to see—like a teenage boy. Isn't an affair supposed to be about gazing into your partner's eyes with a sense of what? she'd wonder, the same emptiness that now defined her?

Maureen steps out of the bathroom. Tom is waiting at the hotel room door, his jacket on.

"I brought you some extra stuff. Just like you asked. It's in the back of the car."

"Thank you. Much appreciated."

"It's ugly out there."

"It is."

Tom pulls on the door handle. The late afternoon sun temporarily blinds her. "Ready?"

A cold breeze prompts Maureen to quickly pull up her winter boots and bundle into her coat.

"Back in a sec." Tom winks, turns, and walks to the motel office.

While she waits for him, Maureen looks behind the driver's seat at the three large plastic bags overflowing with everything she'd asked for: carrots, onions, tomatoes, and spinach. Making a batch of soup to take to the strikers' camp she hopes will somehow fill the empty void. She has heard of parents going off the rails following the loss of a child. She had watched countless talk shows and cable movies about grieving mothers and stoic fathers able to dig deep and find renewed purpose in life before the next commercial break. There will be no prescriptive happy ending in her life. Only the cold emptiness that has dogged her since the day Kenny fell into the river.

Tom slips into the driver's seat.

"Ready?"

"She motions to the bags. "The men will appreciate it."

"Just don't tell them where it came from. I don't think head office would take kindly to knowing that I'm helping to feed the enemy."

"No one will know."

"I was once a card-carrying union member myself. When I first started," he says.

"Can you take me home?"

"'Course."

"I don't want to make you late."

"Don't worry about that. Kate's out and about anyway."

As they drive in silence, she wonders why? Why is she still having sex with a man she was indifferent to in the first place? What about poor, hapless Henry? News of this would—she cannot even come up with a word to describe what it would do to him. Dale? He is easy. As much as he hates his father—simply hates him—he'd come after Tom, pummel him in front of customers, not bothering to think that it takes two to have an affair. She thinks of Kenny. He would be thirteen now, old enough to comprehend what she and Tom have been up to, but not mature enough to understand why. If Kenny were alive, she would never find herself inside room 302 of the Blue Buffalo Motel.

Her hand reaches for the necklace.

"Tom. Stop."

"Stop what?"

"The car."

A combination of impatience and bewilderment crosses his face as he pulls the car to the curb while Maureen frantically pats herself down, wondering if the necklace could have slipped down into her boots.

"I've…" Then she feels it, the dolphin's sharp nose pressing into the fat that folds into her jeans. "I thought I'd lost it."

"Lost…"

"My necklace."

She can tell that Tom does not get it. Not only does he not get it, he is nowhere near to getting it. The necklace to him is nothing more than a cheap silver novelty, probably full of lead. Tom will never know that the dolphin rises and falls with each beat of her heart, as if it were swimming in the white-and-blue waters of a far-off ocean. It keeps it present in her heart that Kenny is floating somewhere up above, in a blue-and-white heaven, or whatever heaven may be.

Pulling the door handle, Maureen cups the fold of fat under her coat with one hand as if she were protective of an unborn child.

She steps out of the car and starts walking toward home.

# THE STRIKE

Standing in the front hallway of Maureen's house, Tom holds up two more bags of vegetables. He's quietly supplying the strikers with food.

"Sorry about yesterday. Did you hear that a bus ran over one of the strikers? Crushed his leg."

"Dale said he almost threw up when he saw it," Maureen replies. She takes the bags and places them on the floor. She crooks her neck, listening for any signs of her son Patrick, who is upstairs getting ready for school. Tom has only been to the house once, when he dropped in during a New Year's Party three years ago, but it's not like Patrick doesn't know who he is. She just doesn't want him wondering why a work colleague would be at the house so early on a weekday morning.

"You still sure you want to do this?" Tom asks. She motions him to step outside into the frigid morning air. "What'd Henry say?"

"I haven't told him. Besides, he and I aren't exactly on speaking terms right now, are we?"

"You're in a tough spot."

"That's putting it mildly."

"I got Steve from the bakery department to throw in some day-old French loaves."

"French? Fancy."

"It all gets tossed anyway. They're in the car."

"Thanks."

"I may be management, but I'm still a union man at heart." He pauses. Stares at her, eyes full of genuine concern. "I want you to be careful."

"What are they going to do? Tear gas a mother for serving soup?"

"I gotta go. Next week?" he asks, his voice hopeful.

The owner of the meatpacking plant where Henry worked had made his first million rolling back odometers on used cars and collecting a series of beautiful women. Boisterous in his admiration of Ayn Rand, he'd pound a battered copy of *Atlas Shrugged* onto the dining-room table at university fraternity houses, espousing the evils of socialism to wide-eyed fraternity boys and future leaders of the province. He had the mayor's ear and a direct line to the premier's office. A well-known and generous political donor, he had a reputation for wringing concessions from every level of government. Times were tough. Tim Tanner knew the cards were in his favour.

When contract negotiations began, Tanner claimed to be cash-poor and told his workers they were lucky to have jobs. All the workers wanted was a small wage increase, plus a boost to the cost-of-living allowance equal to the rate of inflation. It was an open secret that he had dragged out negotiations during the summer, knowing the closer it came to winter the more he would have weather on his side. Henry told Maureen that Tanner planned to lock out the union and bring in scabs. The first day of snow, advertisements for replacement workers appeared in the daily newspapers. A week later, management locked out the workers. Then it began. Maureen knew blood would spill.

=

Henry was apoplectic when Maureen told him of her plans the night before.

"Keep your goddamn nose out where it doesn't belong."

"This is my business."

"You don't know what it's like. They're animals."

"Does that make you an animal too?"

"They're taking to wearing brass knuckles..."

"And the cops are using batons and pepper spray."

"Whose side are you on, anyway?"

"The same side I was on when you went out on strike eight years ago. You sure as hell didn't complain about me bringing you soup then, did you?"

Maureen's face was red with bitterness. She had told Henry not to take the foreman's job, knowing the consequences that union brothers faced when they turn-coated into management. "I curse the day you took that job. I can understand why—we needed the money. But if you hadn't, you'd be out there on the picket line. And I would be doing exactly what I'm doing, supporting the workers like I'd be supporting you. What harm can come of that?"

"You could get me fired."

"I can damn well do whatever I please. Last time I looked this was still a free world."

With that, Maureen turned and stomped her way into the kitchen.

There had been five of them for dinner. Dale brought his girlfriend, Belinda, a doleful girl who'd recently graduated from hairdresser school. Maureen thinks she's useless, a cow without pause, and under her breath calls her a rat-dog because she always appears to be yanking on an invisible leash, yapping, prattling. Constantly complaining about something, she snaps her gum just to let you know she's in the room. True to her vocation, Belinda keeps her hair perfectly coiffed and dyed in the latest colour, her makeup thick to cover potential signs of acne. Her lips always match her polished nails. Belinda is proud of her large breasts, which she shows off by wearing low-cut blouses in the summer or clingy sweaters in the winter. Dale has nicknamed them watermelon one and watermelon two—never to her face and not in the company of others—the exception being Patrick. Patrick wonders how Belinda can cut hair without her watermelons smothering her customers to death. When she's over for the occasional Sunday dinner, he can't help staring at them, especially when she sits directly across from him, those oversized fleshy melons protruding from her chest. She flashes him a coy smile and makes a point of leaning across the table for the potatoes.

Belinda's the first to spread the latest gossip from *Vogue* or *People* magazine. She tells everyone that hairdressing is more than just making people feel good, far more than finding symmetry between the structure of the face and the cut of the hair. Her role is to be a combination fashion and sales consultant and social worker, listening to clients' woes, matrimonial, monetary, and otherwise. She offers expert advice on any and all subjects. Oh, to be nineteen and so worldly.

Maureen watches Henry stew as she washes the dinner dishes, his only comfort being the lukewarm beer that he sips while watching the television. His haggard face confirms the toll the strike is taking on him. Neither of them sleeps as he tosses and turns. She knows what he's thinking. He's concerned for his own safety and for Dale's. He's told Maureen about the gong show inside the plant. With Tanner leaning on him every day, Henry has the impossible task of keeping the production line going. He's even had to man the bolt gun himself to put a cow out of its misery after a replacement worker had badly mangled the job. How hard can it be to level the barrel of a gun against a skull and press the trigger?

After the last plate is dried and put away, Maureen drives the blade of a knife quickly through the onions, carrots, and potatoes Tom had brought her, cursing Henry under her breath, muttering what she'd say if she came face to face with that sonofabitch Tanner. It's not the first time they've been in this situation. Eight years ago, it was different times, different owners. The men went out on strike and Henry was on the outside, on the picket line with his union brethren. The issues were the same. Greed. Money. Ego. Two weeks into it, they settled. Then Tanner bought the place and things changed overnight.

She angles the cutting board over the pot and sweeps the mutilated vegetables into the boiling water. Patrick comes thumping down the stairs and into the kitchen, helping himself to a glass of water before murmuring goodnight and returning to his room. Maureen resists the urge to hug him. He's at an awkward age and avoids motherly affection at all costs. Maureen instead stirs the stock simmering on the stove. Before bed, she carves up the loaves of French bread, lines the slices with mustard and mayonnaise, ham and cheese, before cutting them into hand-sized sandwiches and covering them with plastic wrap.

=

It is still dark when Henry drives through the plant's rear gates. He's never hated this place more than he does now. He hates the livestock, pities the poor souls bawling and mooing at death's door; hates the smell of the piss, shit, and blood; and above all hates the stench of death that clings to him. Alone in his closet-sized office, he drinks coffee and finishes his morning smoke, staring through the glass at the idle production line. The line is no different than any other plant, the hooks, hoses, chains, and pulleys needed to turn a cow into meat. Loath to admit it, he regrets not taking Maureen's advice years ago to get his butcher's ticket. That would've allowed him to work in the meat department at one of the grocery chains. However, although the Safeway and Co-op stores had solid union jobs with better pay and benefits and regular hours, he had no interest in working in a glass zoo, with shoppers staring at him while he carved, sliced, and packaged up meat all day. He thinks of his time as a bolt gunner. The more he did it the more he was cold to killing, until the day came for him to drop the stun gun to become a foreman. Intuitively he knew there was a difference between killing in cold blood and killing something so its carcass could be carved up while hanging from a hook. The same as Henry knew the difference between an owner and a worker. The Tanners of the world saw employees as a means to an end, a commodity to profit from. He remembered how the union reps shook their heads in suspicion when, as a gesture of good faith after he'd bought the company, Tim Tanner introduced a small pension plan. Everyone knew that he did not have an altruistic cell in his body. It was a calculated business decision, a way to ensure longterm work-force stabilty. The longer the workers stayed on the job, the more the tedious, meaningless work carved away their souls. The pension plan was only a further tease into a life of blood and death. The union's call for a boycott of Tanner Meats would be disastrous to the brand and would force the company into bankrupcy soon after the strike was over. An audit would reveal two sets of books: one recording fictitious contributions to the pension plan, the other showing funds being diverted to a numbered company, with Tanner and his wife as sole shareholders.

Henry butts out his cigarette and suddenly thinks of Kenny and how everything changed the day he died. The heart is a series of tectonic plates and Henry's shifted, one plate curling one over the other, the weight of his son's death crushing his spirit. Even to this day, he cannot fathom why Dale could not save him. Henry had been a staunch union man, a shop steward, and a pain in management's ass. He would tell every new pimple-faced worker that if his veins were cut, they'd bleed NDP orange. The day the river swept Kenny's body away, his will to keep up the fight went with it. Why, time and time again he would ask himself after the funeral, why? Why stand up for his working brothers and sisters? Why stand up against unsafe conditions? Why fight the Tanners of the world for common human decency and respect? Or march in the annual Labour Day parade, arms locked in solidary. Why, when at one time you knew you weren't doing it for yourself. You were doing it for them, the next generation of the Kennys, Dales, and Patricks of the world. So, when he was offered the foreman's job, he said fuck it and accepted it. Supervising the line meant that he'd no longer come home every night with blood under his fingernails. He would no longer kill but would watch as others killed.

"I've been offered a foreman's job," he told Maureen and the boys matter-of-factly over the dinner table. "No more cutting n' gutting. Just cracking the whip to keep things going. I git a raise in pay and a production bonus to boot."

Maureen was livid. Dale called him a fucking asshole for turning his back on a union that had supported him over the years.

"You'll not use that language around this house so long as you're living under my roof," Henry roared.

"That can easily change," Dale yelled as he stormed out the front door.

Henry takes a last gulp of his lukewarm coffee as he rises from his desk. He pulls on a clean white smock, wraps and ties the string around this waist, slips on a hairnet, flips the protective white plastic helmet over the hairnet, and heads out to the line. The workers—the scabs—will soon arrive What have I done, he wonders. What have I done?

The night before, Maureen had left a phone message at the union hall, asking for a ride to the strikers' camp. While waiting for the driver to arrive, she sits in the boys' room, her shoulders hunched under the top bunk frame, a necklace in her hand. The bottom bunk was Kenny's. It hasn't been slept in since he died. Patrick refuses to sleep in his dead brother's bed and keeps to the top bunk. Maureen stares at the small dolphin pedant, dulled with age, dangling from its chain. She clasps it around her neck. She doesn't consider herself to be the suspicious type yet every day, more for a lark than anything, she reads her horoscope in the newspaper. She clutches the silver dolphin  as she stares out the bedroom window, knowing what she's doing with Tom is not right. With the strike and her and Henry at each other's throats, things are too complicated right now for her to be fooling around. Is there ever a right time to be going behind your husband's back, she wonders.

Tom had been there for her. He attended the service. The wake. He was waiting for Maureen when she came back for her first shift following her bereavement leave. He pulled her in close for a quick cry before she began. During lunch, he would sit silently while Maureen tried to figure out the bitter fact that Kenny was gone and never coming back.

"I'm afraid for Dale. I don't know what I'm gonna do," she said.

Maureen knew before she began to sleep with Tom that she wasn't the first cashier he had propositioned. He carried his reputation on his shoulders with the same manly pride that he drew on to lift and unpack boxes of fruit and vegetables on the display counters all day long. He suggested that they take their bond to the next level, just after Henry was promoted to foreman, and she quietly accepted. She soon found that, like her husband, Tom lacked the responsiveness and gentle consideration that she desperately wanted. He took his pleasure and didn't notice how half-heartedly Maureen took hers.

The beep of a horn shakes Maureen out of her state. She looks out the bedroom window and sees that an old panel van, its dull sky-blue paint tinged with flecks, is idling beside the curb. A wisp of cigarette smoke curls out from the driver's side. The least he could do is meet her on the front steps, she thinks. Maureen rises, walks down the stairs, and out the door, determined to end things with Tom once and for all.

Sam, the driver, an old-timer at the plant, started well before Henry. Maureen knows him to be a gregarious, joking type who always comes to union socials and meetings alone. He's never married. Rumour has it he spends his weekends at the local after-hours gay nightclub.

"The boys are going to love this," Sam says, as they make their way down the sidewalk. "I'm tempted to have a bowl meself." He places the pot on the truck floor and cushions it with an old pair of pants to minimize the chance of the contents spilling. "Let's put the sandwiches on the back seat ta make sure they stay clean and dry." He gives Maureen a questioning look as he holds the passenger door open for her. Maybe, she thinks, he's not quite sure why she's doing what she's doing, knowing that her husband is on the other side.

"It's Dale's favourite," Maureen says, hoping Sam will make the connection.

"Dale?"

"My son. He's on the picket line."

"Dale? Your oldest boy. Isn't he still in school?"

"School's not for everyone, you know. Some of us are better working with our hands than our heads."

"Must be tough."

"What?"

"You know. Henry being on the inside—"

"Soup's getting cold," Maureen snaps. She climbs into the passenger seat and closes the door.

She's in an impossible position.

Dale was a directionless high-school dropout. After Henry started as a foreman, he pulled some strings and got him a job at the plant. Maureen and Henry both hoped a dead-end job on the processing line would smarten him up enough to get his act together and maybe find an apprenticeship. Henry wasn't surprised when the first thing Dale did after the lockout was to buy a hockey cup and shin and elbow pads. He pulled them out of a paper bag after dinner and goaded his father by holding the cup between his legs. "Let's see those fuckers try and get me in the nuts," he quipped, joking about the riot police that rumours suggested would show up first thing in the morning to escort buses full of scab workers through the plant gates.

Dale had a reputation for youthful impulsiveness. He found freedom in fighting. When he was in school, his parents had been called to the principal's office on more than one occasion when his temper tantrums in grade school got the better of him. Things only got worse when he reached high school. Adolescent fisticuffs soon gave way to barroom and back-alley brawls. No matter if he won or not, Dale loved being in the middle of it all. Even when down for the count, he'd have to be restrained from getting up for a second pummelling. When he fought, he seemed blind to the blood and indifferent to the pain. What Dale lacked in finesse, he made up with wild abandon, muscle, and a willingness to jump into the fray at a moment's notice.

Dale got quickly sucked into the whole union thing—the solidarity of brothers and sisters in arms and workers' rights. Us versus them. He read the union bulletin board in the lunchroom every day and religiously attended the monthly meetings down at the union hall. Afterward, he sat around with his brothers and sisters, eager to listen as they bitched about working conditions, money, spouses, and children. He lapped up the stories of Cesar Chavez and how he organized farm workers in California and was in awe of the union local's president, Jimmy Stewart, who spoke enviously of the strength of organized labour in the industrial heartland to the east and in the forestry and mining sectors in British Columbia. One weekend he even tried listening to Woody Guthrie and Bob Dylan, but rock'n'roll got in the way.

As the van nears the plant, it passes the police staging area.

"Rat bloody police union," Sam spits out, nodding to the grim-faced riot police huddled together, helping one another don Kevlar gloves and rib protectors. "They're in their fucking element just ready to lay a beating on anyone within reach."

Police dogs whine, pace excitedly in the backseats of waiting cruisers. A cop stands atop of a cube van with a video camera mounted on a tripod. Others joke and jostle. Shield their bravado behind Plexiglas face masks. A policeman, tall, as wide as a football player, stares and smiles at Maureen as he slaps a baton into his gloved hand. Arrogant bastard, she thinks. You wouldn't hesitate to crack me over the head, would you?

"The only difference between a bouncer and a cop is a badge," Sam says.

He pulls the van to a stop in an empty lot near the plant gates where the union's erected a small camp of warming tents, port-a-potties, a soup kitchen, an open-air resting area, and a first aid tent. Despite Tim Tanner's best efforts, the city fathers have taken a conciliatory position. Maureen spots Dale with fellow strikers around a burning oil drum, warming his hands while stomping his feet on the frozen ground. They're sharing coffee and doughnuts as they talk amongst themselves. One looks nervously from his watch to the plant gates where the picket line is slowly growing. As she steps from the van, Maureen gets everyone's attention  by waving at the policeman with the video camera. The strikers chuckle, amused by her small act of defiance.

"Maureen Fitzpatrick. So good to see you. Even if your husband is an arsehole," a striker shouts.

"Now, now, Carl. You can't put all the blame on Henry. He's just doing his job. And you'd be doing the same if you were a white shirt," she replies. "If there's anyone to blame it's that goddamn Tim Tanner," she says to no one in particular. "Now let's get something warm into yous. Let it simmer on the Coleman," she orders Sam, pointing to the portable gas stove on a metal stand outside the tent door. Dale has remained at the fire, hands wrapped firmly around a steaming Styrofoam cup. He takes a step in Maureen's direction, but she waves him off. There's plenty of help with fresh soup coming.

As Maureen stirs the pot and unpacks the sandwiches, Jimmy Stewart arrives in his truck. He steps out, making momentary eye contact with Maureen before turning away to rouse the troops. Right up to the day that Henry traded a blue shirt for a white one, Jimmy used to be friends and drinking buddies with him. They were close enough that Jimmy's wife, Carol, and Maureen used to be friends. They would team up for the annual union bowling tournament. It was always a hoot. They and the other men got drunker than skunks, falling on their arses after guttering the ball. The only option left to their wives and girlfriends was to take them home. Maureen and Henry no longer go to the bowling tournament. Or the summer union barbeque. Jimmy has barely spoken to Henry since he started his foreman's job and when the two men do speak, they limit themselves to pleasantries and union-management issues. Henry is management. A pariah.

Midway up a hill overlooking the plant, Archie Cunningham positions himself in a small copse of trees, confident that the hunting jacket he's purchased at the thrift store will provide the necessary camouflage. Twice he scouted this location, his anger building both times he watched the bus carrying the replacement workers again go through the gates. He doesn't want to hurt anyone. He just wants to make them think twice about quitting welfare or their taxi-driving job to become scabs. Before the lockout, things were looking up for Archie. For months he'd been bugging Henry Fitzpatrick to give him a chance as a bolt-gun operator. Henry told him to be patient, that his time would come. Everyone knew the bolt-gun operator was a big man in the shop. Anyone who could kill with the blink of an eye for forty hours a week, fifty weeks of the year, was given a wide berth. Archie doesn't see any difference between butchering a cow and shooting rabbits in the woods with an arrow like he'd done when he was a kid. Dead was dead. He's certain that all Fitzpatrick was doing was pulling his chain. The more Archie bugged him, the more impatient the foreman got.

"Give your fucking balls a tug and wait your turn," Henry told him.

Then he got locked out.

What Archie really wants to do is put a bolt gun to Tim Tanner's head and pull the trigger. But it's not just Tanner. The union has lied too.

"It'll be over in a week. Two at the most," he'd heard Jimmy Stewart boast, first at the union hall, then to the media on the first day of the strike. "We'll bring 'em to the bargaining table. You'll see."

So Archie has developed a plan. He'll scare the bejesus out of those brown-boy scabs from African countries and cities with names he can't even find on a map, never mind pronounce— Samallia? Mogadishwho?—he'll make those fuckers think twice about taking good union jobs from real Canadians.

Clouds form from the herd of breathing men who gather seeking instructions. Men with arms as thick as logs and a thirst for beer and justice, wearing toques and Oilers caps, their bodies warm with worn winter jacket and thick flannel lumberjack shirts, their skin damp under their clothes, gather in preparation for the daily battle. Jockstraps and cups are worn over blue jeans.

Old Spice, coffee, and whiskey waft into the air. Fists are wrapped around brass knuckles. There is a mutual desperation amongst them, a worthiness in their brutality. They are the lowest of the low, expendable. Banks, insurance companies, funeral directors see them only for what little money they have.

Union leaders whip them into a frenzy.

A sudden stillness fills the air. The faint rhythmic bang of batons against shields—*thrump, thrump, thrump*—gets louder with each beat. With each beat of the batons, something buried deep inside, a collective primordial urge—the urge to kill—is awoken.

Maureen reflexively turns and sees the policeman on the roof of cube van roof swing his camera The strikers rush to the plant gates. Some wear hockey helmets and protect their teeth with mouth guards. Small knives and screwdrivers for slashing tires and skin glint in the morning light. Baseball bats appear. Steel-mesh gloves are pulled on. Dale gets swept up in the crush, but suddenly he stops and turns to his mother. With a childlike smile, he forms a gun with his fingers and motions to his groin as if to reassure her that the family jewels are safe behind his hockey cup.

Like medieval warriors, two rows of riot police march shoulder to shoulder, and are so thickly bound, a thread would not pass between them. A school bus, its yellow lights rhythmically blinking, follows closely behind. The front windshield is covered in steel mesh, the side windows are blacked out. Police in full riot gear, batons and pepper spray at the ready, line each side of the bus. As Maureen watches it pass, she thinks of a television show. A thick-chested instructor with a southern drawl, his hair cropped Marine-short and his white T-shirt tucked in tight, illustrated the proper use of police riot gear: a quick jab of a baton to the quadriceps and into bicep nerve-clusters causes searing muscle pain, instant weakness, spasms, and temporary paralysis; cayenne-pepper spray renders an antgonist vulnerable to fists and boots as the subject flails away, eyes burning and lungs choking.

Maureen searches for Dale. He's disappeared into a sea of stone-faced workers, chins held high, chests pumped, muscles flexed, men who stand man to man, shoulder to shoulder, brother to brother, blocking the plant entrance. Outnumbered and outgunned, they know their greatest weapon is not their fists and feet but the court of public opinion. The men are defiant in their defence for working men across the country. In further defiance, all but a few are still wearing company-issued steel-toed boots.

"Fucking scabs."

"Paki cocksuckers."

"Rot in hell, motherfuckers."

"Scabs."

"Go back to driving a taxi."

"Go back where you came from, ya fucking jigaboos."

Macho superiority courses through their veins. Oozes into the  winter air with every breath.

Maureen cranes her head as she moves toward the gate. A hand, solid and strong, grips her left shoulder.

"Stay back, Maureen," Sam says, his voice gentle but firm. "For your own good."

An eerie calm blankets the factory site.

The police commander steps forward, legs splayed wide. He reads the injunction aloud, knowing it will fall on deaf ears. This is a province where there are two types of men; men, and men who make their money off the backs of other men.

The police stand stone-faced, knowing that strikers' children go to school without breakfast; are taunted by other kids; that predatory bill collectors are phoning mothers with threatening voices. Already one striker has committed suicide. Wives are taking second minimum-wage jobs to put food on the table.

The idea of union solidarity evaporates when the police unions face other unions.

The strikers stand, defiant.

Dale sweeps the hair out of his eyes. A smile erupts on his face.

"What about our rights?" a voice demands.

"Fuck you," another is heard from somewhere deep in the crowd.

A worker raises his arm in defiance.

The commander gives the strikers one minute to disperse. As he turns, a rock flies through the air, hitting him in the shoulder. The strikers surge forward, punching and clawing, attempting to throw themselves into the bus's path. Police dogs bark and excitedly yap, itching for blood. A striker takes a swing with a baseball bat. A Plexiglas shield deflects the blow, and the man is gang tackled. He slumps to the ground, attacked by cops hungry for revenge. Faces are smashed. Arms broken. Abdomens implode from the blunt impact of the truncheons. Breath is cut off. Men bleed. Cry. Vomit. Scream. The lone woman in the melee, a tough Russian immigrant, delivers a blow to a cop's ribs. He grunts, surprised by the power of her punch. A cop slams a baton into the wrist of a striker who has brought out a knife, breaking his bones. He keeps hammering as the striker falls to the ground. The man lacks the time and strength to protect his head as he hurls to the asphalt where his flesh is flayed and his skull cracked. A Molotov cocktail lands harmlessly near the holding pen where livestock moo at the chaos. A striker, prone on the ground, is trampled. Another is beaten about the face while two cops hold his arms. A cop kicks the knees out from under a worker before smacking him in the ribs with his truncheon. Bloodied fists and broken placards pound the side of the bus. Minutes pass. Men pant and snarl, exulting in their tango of brutality.

The bus inches forward as fallen bodies are dragged to the sidelines. Inside, men, many of whom do not speak English, drop to the floor, as far away from the windows as possible, unaware that they are mere pawns in a capitalist battle. They cringe, holding their hands over their heads as the bus is pelted with rocks, hit with lengths of lumber and with whatever else the strikers can get their hands on. Few comprehend the racist rants, yet they all recognize the heat in the bitter, angry words and in the fists that pound the bus.

Dale swings his fists fiercely. Rocking on one foot, the guy beside him catches a cop in the balls with a steel-toed boot and is immediately taken down. Out of principle, he keeps hammering away until he is pulled back by two workers.

It is one-sided, a David vs. Goliath affair. The outcome a foregone conclusion. The towel is thrown in. Police and strikers retreat to their corners. They all watch, exhausted as the bus passes. A weak "we showed 'em" cheer rises from the strikers. They snarl at the retreating police and let out a celebratory hooray, knowing the only measure of their success is in the damage done—a broken windshield, a slashed tire, an injured cop, and that the only thing this daily clash will accomplish will be the headline it will create in the newspapers and the lead story on the evening news.

The strikers retreat, defiant, bloody, and bruised to the camp, the healthy assisting those with broken bones and split skin as a fresh line of strikers man the picket line. A few hork out coagulated blood from their bloodied mouths and noses that splatters onto the vermillion-dusted snow.

There is a shifting in the air. A cloud passes over the winter moon and the frigid wind picks up, freezing the beading blood on open wounds. Later, with the pain still running up to their throats, some will rub their bruised balls until it passes, hoping a visit to the hospital will not be in order. Bandages and ice will cover blackend eyes and open wounds. They will dull their pain, lick their wounds with liquor. Stitches will pull split skin together and the scars will be something to be shared with grandchildren.

Dale plops into a ribbed aluminum chair inside the first-aid tent, a bloodied cloth to his head. Maureen pushes the tent flap aside and joins him.

"What mischief have you got yourself into this time?" she asks with a hint of humour as she bends down on one knee.

"I cold-cocked a fucking cop…"

"Language please…"

"…right in the nuts."

"I'm still your mother," she says.

"They tried to gang-tackle me. But I got away."

"Let me see."

Dale grins as he allows her to pull the cloth from his head. She emits a whooshing sound at the sight of blood oozing from his temple.

"You need stitches."

"The second I leave, the cops will arrest me."

"They'll have to go through me first."

"Mom…"

"This isn't the first time I've done this, you know. You forget your father walked this same picket line eight years ago. Back then, I got vegetables from the food bank and brought a pot of soup once a week. It was the least I could do then. It's the least I can do now."

"Look at him. Fucking…"

"Shush with the language. You stay here. I'll come back with some soup. That'll warm you up. I'll take some to the boys. Then I'll talk to Jimmy. See what he can do about keeping you out of jail. It's not like the cops are lily-white angels in all of this."

Archie watches as the workers limp to the camp. Scab replacement workers scramble from the bus and scurry through the plant doors. The riot police retreat to the command post. He locks the sleek aluminum arrow into position. With its double-barbed steel points strategically located behind the head, the arrow is designed for maximum efficiency. He knows that if he wanted to, he could creep down close and in a second pierce the bus's sheet metal, but he still has an outstanding warrant in Ontario and doesn't want to risk getting caught. The plan is to aim the arrow so it lands just inside the front gates where the scabs gather at the end of their shift before boarding the bus to go home. The ground is frozen, so it won't penetrate the ground. As dramatic as it would be to lodge its tip in the ground, the message the arrow will send is more important. To make it clear who the arrow's intended target is, Archer has etched "scab" crudely into the aluminum.

He tests the wind with his finger to mentally calculate the angle. He studies the curl of grey-black smoke from the burning oil drum as it drifts slowly westward. Perfect. He leans back and aims the crossbow at the clouds, inhales and holds his breath as his grandfather had taught him, his index finger curled around the trigger. A glint of white light reflecting off something below distracts him. Archie lowers the crossbow. Exhales. The cop on top of the cube van has his video camera pointed directly at him. Archie collapses into the snow, his face cold, less from the bitter wind than from the sweat evaporating on his exposed skin. His heart thumps hard and fast inside his chest as he watches the cop complete a final pan of the area. He turns and looks uphill, half expecting to see a throng of police to come swarming over its crest. He closes his eyes, breathes deeply, knowing that the greatest asset a hunter has is patience. His breathing causes the pounding in his chest to subside.

Archie watches as the cop climbs into the cab of the cube van and drives away. As it disappears, he takes one last look at the scene below. Things have settled down. A woman carrying a bowl exits the tent. A man follows and places a steaming pot in a kid's red wagon.

"Made fresh this morning," Maureen says as she hands Dale the bowl of soup. "It'll warm you from the inside out."

"Thanks." Dale grins, raises the bowl of soup, and offers his mother a puckish smile from a son not quite ready to grow up.

Maureen looks at Carl. He's standing beside the wagon, with one hand firmly on the pot. "You got it, Carl." He gives her a thumbs up. "We got 'er, Maureen."

Maureen begins to pull the wagon across the packed snow toward a group of men huddling around the fire.

Archie steadies himself against a tree. As he squeezes the trigger, a gust of wind slams into his right cheek. As it barrels into the sky, the arrow drifts through the cloud of ice crystals formed by his breath. Archie curses, watching the arrow as it spins on its axis, propelled through the air, angling off course. Archie predicts it will now land on the public side of the fence, but safely away from the strikers. As it reaches the apex of its vertical trajectory, it comes to a momentary pause. The weight of the head dips it down. Its tail warbles with a second gust of wind. As the arrow veers ever so slightly, spearing into a fast, deep dive, winging farther and further from his original target, Archie scrambles up the hill and is soon out of sight.

Maureen pauses to catch her breath. "You okay, Carl?"

"Just fine, Maureen. Just fine."

"I'm getting too old for this strike business." She looks back at Dale and smiles. "A trade'll sort him out. Union or not."

Dale looks at her. He knows she loves him and Patrick, maybe as much as she did Kenny. Dale inhales the steaming soup deep into his lungs. It sends a warm tingle down his spine. Briefly dulls the throbbing that the baton to his temple has caused. He shakes his head. Yet again, she's taken his side. He can't count the number of times she's done this. Swallowed her pride and asked for forgiveness on behalf of her sons. His transgressions have never been the serious sort—nothing to get him thrown into juvenile detention like Patrick's friend, Lance Mueller, or into jail like Lance's older brother. His were more the usual teenage mischief stuff—shoplifting, fighting, skipping school. He has always been more proud than ashamed—shame and embarassment was only felt when he had to face his mother when she got wind of his adolescent shenanigans. The worst he's done is to try to pawn off a hunting rifle he'd stolen from an ex-girlfriend's house. That's when his mother said she'd had enough. "I don't have the time for this," she told him. "I really don't." Dale promised not to get into trouble again, but trouble always seemed to follow Dale.

A sickening oomph resounds across the camp. The arrow angles through Maureen's breast, between her ribs and out her back, its force pushing her backwards onto her heels. She stares at Dale wide-eyed, her arms held out in front of her. Her head bobbles. Snaps right. Curls left, her jaw slack. She tries to speak, yet only a guttural sound comes out. Dale spills the hot soup onto his lap as he scrambles to his feet.

"Mom...Mom..."

He cannot fathom what the thin silver pencil protruding from the front and back of her torso is. "Mom!" he screams.

Maureen's eyes roll to the back of her head, her face wan. She tries reaching for the arrow but in the wind her fingers flutter. She falls to her knees, knocking the pot off the red wagon. Her forehead cracks as she collapses to the frozen ground. Chunks of chicken bounce across the snow-grey surface. Yellow noodles squirm around her. Her jeans sop up the oily broth. Blood oozes from the hole just below her rib cage. Broth and blood turn the snow pink.

Dale drops to his knees. His body shakes. He gazes at his mother gasping as a stream of blood continues to pulsate from the wound in her chest. Around him thunder shrill yells, syncopated cries and whispers, the panicked shriek of a man on a walkie-talkie. Dale gazes into the sky and screams for help.

Men stand in shock, hands frozen to their mouths.

"Get Henry out here," Jimmy Stewart shouts into his walkie-talkie. "Tell 'em it's Maureen. And get an ambulance. Now."

"Where's First Aid? Where's the fuckin' First Aid attendant?" someone yells.

A minute later, Henry rushes out of the plant to the gate.

"Open the gate. Open the fucking gate," he screams at the security guard.

He rushes over and kneels beside Dale, who's shivering and gasping for air. Henry tries to place a hand on Dale's shoulder but it's shaken off in a flush of anger.

"Don't touch me. Don't ever touch me again," Dale hisses, his eyes brimming with tears.

"Maureen," Henry whispers. "Maureen."

He half-rises on his knees, frantic. "Where's the ambulance? Where's the fucking ambulance?" he screams. "Can anyone help?" Henry watches Stephen Lundy, the shop First Aid attendant, ferret his way through the crowd, his face ashen.

"My kit," he says. "It's inside."

"You," Jimmy Stewart points to a striker. "Go get his kit."

Lundy mumbles his ABCs—"airway, breathing, circulation"—under his breath as drops to his knees beside Henry. "On her side... before she drowns in her own blood," he says.

Lundy carefully rolls her on her right side. Dale and Henry cover her with their coats.

The police commander pushes his way through the crowd, barking cop code into his radio as the wail of the approaching ambulance grows louder. "We need an escort."

Two paramedics hatch out of the ambulance. They pull their gurney, loaded with tools of the trade—a defibrillator, ventilator, devices used to stave off death. Their faces remain neutral. The senior of the two bends on knees that crack.

"What's her name?" he asks nobody in particular.

"M... Maureen Fitzpatrick," Henry replies. "She's my wife,"

"Maureen, can you hear me?" he says. "My name is John. We're going to take care of you. Can you open your eyes? Can you hear me?" his voice growing louder.

The paramedics break into a well-rehearsed action, monitor her vital signs.

"Bolt cutters. Anybody got bolt cutters? We need to cut this thing off," the younger one of the two demands.

The paramedics barely exchange a word, speak instead with eyes grave with concern.

A scab sprints from the plant carrying bolt cutters and blankets. He surrenders the tool and freezes, gazing around warily, suddenly realizing he's in enemy territory. He slowly retreats to the safety of the gate.

The paramedics cut away the head and tail of the arrow and hand them to the police commander.

As Maureen is loaded into the ambulance, Dale jumps in beside her. He glares at his father. "You go with the cops."

The "*we-you, we-you*" of the siren fades into the cold crisp air, as the ambulance crawls over ice.

Dale braces himself against the vehicle's rhythmic sway, lest he fall into Maureen. Her blood, caked on his hands, has glued his fingers together. He stares at her with tear-filled eyes, blinking away a stream of his own blood that trickles down the side of his face. He instinctively wipes it away and covers his mouth with his hand. The metallic smell of Type A and Type O blood coagulating as one flares his nostrils. The attendance offers a handi-wipe but it's impossible to wipe his hands in a rocking vehicle and keep his balance.

"We're almost there," he says. "Hang on, please, Mom, hang on."

Dale brushes a wisp of hair from her forehead. Her skin is cold. He tells her that he loves her, that Patrick and Henry love her. He promises her he'll change. He'll be a good boy. He'll quit the fighting and the drinking. He'll find a job, find a girl. Settle down.

"You've always wanted to be a grandmother," he whispers. "Just don't leave me," he pleads. "Just don't leave me. Not now. Not ever."

Dale gazes through the small skylight in the ceiling of the ambulance knowing that God or Jesus or whoever the hell else is up there fucking with them again. First Kenny. Now his mother? Who do you think you are? he silently demands, knowing he is losing her, his wish nothing more than a winter miracle. He looks at the senior attendant for any signs of hope. The paramedic purses his lips, stares at the monitors, fiddles with the oxygen mask.

"We're almost there," the junior paramedic says.

Dale gazes at his mother. Her chest looks still. The only sounds she makes are the gurgles struggling from under the mask. The siren wails. The air pulses red and blue. As the ambulance nears the hospital, Maureen exhales her final breath.

# MOURNING

Patrick stares at the woman standing beside the school principal. She is wearing a police uniform. Red piping runs down each pantleg. Her brown hair is cropped short. She gives Patrick a sympathetic look.

There has been an...incident," the principal says, his voice sombre. "Constable Mackenzie is here to take you home."

A razor slits at Patrick's heart. It must be Dale, he thinks. His older brother is picketing outside the meat plant where he works. His father is working inside. He's not allowed to go out on strike like he used to when he was part of the union. And Mom? She's at home.

The constable clears her throat. Patrick swallows the urge to cry as she lays a gentle hand on his shoulder. She leads him down the hallway to the school's main entrance, outside through the empty playground, and to her waiting cruiser.

Patrick crawls in and presses his small frame against the dark blue vinyl bench seat. The crackled voice on the police radio, which squeaks and rattles from somewhere inside the car, and the woman's attempt at small talk come from somewhere in the distance. Tires bump over potholes. The rack and shush of the cruiser weaving through traffic bounces him around.

"Sorry," the woman says.

=

Dale, his eyes red, is waiting at the curb when the car arrives. The woman acknowledges him with a silent nod. She gets out to open the door for her passenger. "Take care, Patrick. You too, Dale." Patrick is not surprised that she knows his brother's name. Their father, just like his own father when he was young, had had to bail him out of jail a couple of times.

"Thanks," Dale says, his voice quietly respectful. He takes a deep breath, careful to avoid Patrick's gaze.

"What…" Patrick begins.

"Not here." He motions to the front door. "Inside." As they walk up the sidewalk, Dale bows his arm across his brother's back.

The living room is worn. The odour of stale tobacco lingers in the air, sticks to the furniture. Henry sits on the edge of the couch, his work clothes smelling of meat and bone. He rises, getting only as far as "your mother" before collapsing back onto the couch cushions. The three of them fall forward into a huddle, arms draped over shoulders. After a moment and without a word, the huddle is broken.

Patrick retreats to the couch. Henry slumps back down beside him, the grey winter light blanketing his face in a grey sheen. Bristles of black hair curl from his nose. Patrick feels the heat rising from his father, introducing an unfamiliar intimacy. He watches as Dale leans forward in the worn chair near the kitchen, his elbows on his knees as he plucks at a tissue with his fingernails. Patrick looks past him at a teacup that sits on the counter near the sink. He half-expects to see his mother rattling around the kitchen, banging pots and pans, putting away dishes, before sipping on her tea and asking why all the glum faces.

Henry clears his throat and rises, his man smell wafts from his armpits. "I'd better make some phone calls," he says, his voice quiet.

Dale curls his fingers into the arms of the chair, rising to his feet. "You killed her so you might as well bury her too. Right?"

"I didn't… I didn't kill her. I didn't shoot the arrow that killed her. I told, I told her not to come near the plant. But Maureen being Maureen, she wouldn't listen."

Dale stands and squares up this father. His right hand curls into a fist. Henry pulls the phone off the side table and holds it protectively in front of him as Dale jams a finger within an inch of his face.

"Stay the fuck outta my way."

Dale turns and rushes out the front door, slamming it behind him. Patrick follows his brother's lead and retreats upstairs to his bedroom.

=

Mourning, Patrick finds, is not a steady state but waves of the same storm. Sobs shake him from head to heel; a coldness numbs the tips of his hands and toes in between flashes of warmth and an emptiness that only sleep can lull.

He spends the days leading up to the funeral alone in his room. The long light of January's short day filters through brittle leaves that remain on the tree outside his bedroom as they curl and flutter in the winter wind. He stares out the window and listens to the chortling of magpies, the distant blaring of horns and backfiring trucks, while murmuring voices rise from downstairs as neighbours and friends come and go.

At night, Patrick dreams of his mother. Sometimes she's at the stove making roast beef and potatoes for Sunday dinner. Sometimes she's ironing while watching the soaps or she's sitting with her feet on the coffee table, warmed by a pair of hand-knitted purple slippers and a half-eaten roll of her favourite treat— chocolate digestive cookies—beside her, cigarette in one hand, cup of tea in the other. In the morning, he looks around his bedroom, often thinking of the time he helped his mother scrape off the worn wallpaper before they went to the paint store to search through the discontinued bin for new paper. He thinks of the times he was ordered to sit in the small red plastic chair in the corner of the kitchen—punishment for yet another childish misdeed. She'd watch him askance while she made supper, watching him watching her—and yes, she always forgave him. Please come back, he pleads in his dreams. Please come back and I will sit in the chair again. When the urge to pee wakes him, Patrick passes his parents' bedroom on the way to the bathroom. Most nights his father's lying supine on his bed, staring at the ceiling, her wedding ring in his hand.

When the house is empty, Patrick walks around wrapped in a deep-blue blanket covered in sports figures. He thinks of last August when he and his friends went to the neighbourhood swimming pool. They jumped in feet first, sank to the bottom, worming for balance as their noses billowed bubbles. It was a test to see who could stay on the bottom the longest while the sounds of their summer world—feet kicking, water splashing, swimmers' laughter, and screams above the warnings of the lifeguards—failed to reach them through the clear water.

=

This is the private part of the service, a liminal moment allowing immediate family to pay their final respects. Except for Henry, Patrick, Aunt Jenny, and a funeral-home employee who stands near the doorway—one hand over the other, head bowed, jaw pushed dutifully into his neck to form a doughy collar of marshmallow skin—the room is empty. When the doors open, mourners and sympathizers known and unknown, who have gathered on the street will pour in. There will be the ritual condolences—solemn women bearing tissues, thuggish, salt-of-the-earth working-class men offering a reassuring hug or punch to the shoulder.

Little will be said because nothing more will need to be said.

Patrick stands in front of the coffin beside Jenny. He rubs each shoe against the back of his legs. He glances up at his aunt out of the corner of his eye. She has a disposition that fits seamlessly onto a jowly face that masks an ungentle sadness. She is more square than rectangular. Her ankles and wrists are thick. A wattle of skin hangs under her chin from ear to ear. When Patrick hugged Jenny after she arrived, she smelled of cigarette smoke. A whiff of urine confirmed that she has been drinking. A few years ago, the morning after a night of drinking around the kitchen table, Maureen told Patrick that the sister-in-law she'd tolerated more than liked and who'd earned the nickname Gin-n-tee in her twenties, had recently developed a sensitive bladder.

Jenny keeps repeating to him, "What are we going to do with you?" "Whatever are we going to do with you?"

A cramp seizes Patrick's calf muscle. His neck and shoulders ache. He swallows, forcing his tongue to the top of his mouth, fearing that he might suffocate. He quivers, thrusting out his lower lip involuntarily. Polyester fumes from the shirt Aunt Jenny bought him for the funeral waft up his nose. Factory folds carve into the base of his spine. The front folds over the cowboy belt his mother gave him the Christmas before. Henry told Patrick that Jenny bought the shirt thinking he'd grow into it. Working-class pragmatism. Nor has she children of her own. She should have known her sister-in-law would not allow her boys to wear anything that did not fit. You can be poor, his mother used to say, but you do not have to show it.

Jenny brushes away a strand of stringy hair that hangs across her face. Her plastic rainbow-coloured bracelets clack together. She grips her nephew's hand, squeezing harder than necessary—as if to reassure them both while assuaging their mutual sorrow. She looks over at him and offers up a mirthless smile, her eyes sad in the knowledge that the helpless are beyond help.

"It's okay," she whispers, "Dale would never miss his mother's funeral now, would he?"

Of course, he won't, Patrick thinks. He'll be here. He said he would.

Patrick pushes the toes of his shoes into the thick velvety carpet and arches the small of his back. His pants ride above his ankles, exposing tube socks that accordion his legs. Jenny gives him a curious glance. He wonders what would happen if he accidentally slipped forward into the coffin. Would the attendant in the black suit, who stands sombre and respectful at the back of the room, his greased-back black hair polished by the artificial light, walk calmly over with a white cloth to wipe his fingerprints from the finely polished wood? Would his father grab him by the scruff of the neck and pull him into an adjoining room in order to take his pain out on him?

=

Maureen is white. Silent. Her cheeks are sunken. Her hair, streaked with grey where the jaw meets the skull, is stiff with spray. Rouge gloss waxes her lips. The skin of her neck has settled into her cabled throat. Eyelashes perch on collapsed lids. A fleck of makeup, thinner than a wafer, stands straight on the bridge of her nose. Her left hand rests over her right, glued together peacefully. Henry insisted that she be dressed in her wedding dress. It is off-white, strapless, cut low. Maureen had picked it off the department store sale rack and it was altered by a friend. Patrick wonders how the funeral people managed to squeeze her into something she'd worn before she had children. Had they left it undone at the back where no one can see? Are her feet bare under the coffin lid? Her breasts, flat, hide a heart that was broken by so many others.

More than anything, Patrick wants to put his head on his mother's chest. With each passing moment her voice becomes lighter, the feel of her hugs feathery, her pearly green eyes glassy. He tilts his head forward. A fly lands on her forehead above the left eye. It makes Patrick think of the time she told him that the freckles on his face were fly poop. The *gotcha* smile that followed reassured him that she was joking. At school, Patrick's teacher told the class that maggots are fly larvae. Will the fly lay eggs on his mother's eyes? Doesn't the fly know that she will be cremated, and its eggs will burn with her? Jenny shoos it away with her hand. The draft created by the flick of her wrist catches the fleck of makeup. It wavers and pirouettes. A tiny ballerina.

He stares at one of two tables near the entrance to the room. It overflows with bright and sombre cards; wreaths of flowers; stuffed animals—playful bunnies with big brown eyes, fat blue-eyed cats, and long-eared, droopy dogs. On the second table, a white book of condolences lies open beside a white feathered pen in a cheap white plastic stand.

Patrick watches as the funeral director slips through the door. He is short, balding, and droll-looking, with saggy jowls and a small tight mouth, serious eyes, and a black mole just below his left temple. Dressed in a dark-blue suit, he tugs on his right sleeve as his eyes sweep the room, pausing on Patrick long enough to give him a sympathetic smile. He acknowledges the attendant with a coded gaze. Taps his watch with his index finger. The director's smile slips into a frown. Motioning to Henry, he strides across the room. The two men step away from the casket and huddle. The director strokes his jaw. Henry leans into him. Patrick overhears bits and pieces of the conversation—a second service, the gathering crowd, a schedule to keep. The director glides his right hand between Henry's shoulder blades back before stepping away, palms open Jesus-like. Suffer little children. Henry nods, not questioning the director's instructions, knowing that a funeral, like a kill line, must function efficiently.

"They'll open the doors in five minutes," Henry whispers to no one in particular. "They're all waiting outside. The mayor. Members of city council. The director says he's heard that even the premier might show up."

"I don't give a rat's ass about any politician. Where were they when this was all happening?" Jenny asks, her voice huffy.

"Where do you think they were? Standing around with their heads up their asses," Henry said, his voice bitter.

Patrick hadn't realized till now that the public nature of his mother's murder would require a public response and elected officials to offer platitudes. Why else would these people, who wouldn't give the time of day to a woman who worked as a cashier, make an appearance? To be seen at a funeral is no different than cutting a ribbon to open a new community centre.

Patrick is determined to take what there is to be had from empty words proffered by a stranger of the cloth, who will ask everyone present to raise their hearts and find solace in the Bible and Jesus Christ, about whom Patrick has heard little, knows little, and has no desire to believe in. Later, alone in his room, he will empty his pockets and try to make sense of it all.

"What about...," Patrick begins.

"I can't do anything about him, now can I?" Henry hisses quietly.

"But..."

"If he's here, he's here. If not . . ."

Patrick knows Dale won't miss the service. Any minute now he'll walk through the door and stand beside him. Protect him.

Whisper in his ear and tell him what to do. He'll give Patrick a wink and a nod if Patrick picks his nose. Nudge him in the ribs if Patrick's about to scratch his crotch. That's what big brothers do. They look out for you. Put you in your place when you need to be put in your place.

Dale will give him a hug for the sake of a hug before telling him not to be a baby. He used to goad Patrick with a flick of a finger to his ear or provoke him to the point of tears. Their mother's glare always convinced Dale to pull back. Yet he also gave Patrick his only pair of skates. They were CCM Tacks, the Rolls Royce of hockey skates—two sizes too big. The blades were dull, the leather faded and worn. Rust had formed around the rivets where blade and boot bonded. When their father asked him where he got the skates, Dale merely shrugged.

Smelling of beer and cigarettes, Dale would sometimes saunter into Patrick's bedroom and signal for him to shift over before flopping down beside him. The time that Patrick asked what working at the plant was like, a stern looked crossed Dale's face.

"Everyone, including me and the old man, we're losers. Just fucking losers. We're no more alive than the livestock coming down the kill chute. You go into a place like that alive and come out dead. There's no way I'm gonna be a lifer. Not like the old man. What Belinda says is true. I have to figure out what I want to do with my life. Pick up a trade maybe. But you—you promise me," he said, tapping Patrick's temple with the tip of his finger. "You got something up there. Use it. Don't become like us. And don't you ever, ever, set a fucking foot in that plant. Got it?"

Patrick nodded.

"Good. Otherwise I'd be forced to kill ya," he said, bumping his head on the bunk rail as he rose. "And I wouldn't want to do that 'cause you're my little brother."

Otherwise he mostly shared details about his latest fight with his girlfriend, joking that Belinda isn't *the* girl, just a *will-do-for-now* kind of girl.

Patrick fidgets, less out of disrespect for his mother and more out of a desire to finally have her death over with so he can join his friends, out in the cold, and play street hockey or wander around the river valley. His friends are there for him, like always. Lance left an Oh Henry! chocolate bar in the mailbox, wrapped in a yellow smiley-face note. Jennifer's two moms left a casserole.

"We've only got a few minutes, Patrick. You should give your mother a kiss," Jenny says. "She would like that." She looks at him. "Go on."

"I have to…" Patrick says, his voice small, signifying a more urgent matter.

Jenny nods. "All right, but make it quick."

Patrick pivots on his heels while his father runs a finger along the casket's bevelled edge.

"Maybe we should've gone maple rather than the oak."

"Too late now," Jenny says to Henry.

A vase of white silk lilies stands on the bathroom counter. Patrick stands in front of the urinal. He closes his eyes and listens to the tinkling of his urine against the porcelain, wondering how the woman who bore him could be gone so suddenly. His vision blurred by tears on the night of her death, he stared out his bedroom window at the waxing moon and the stars. Somewhere out there, he'd thought, she was, an abstract face framed in a blue grey cloud. Life was no longer as it had been days before.

Patrick is thankful that the service will soon be over. He will be able to go home to a bed that hasn't been made for days. He will close his eyes and cry one final time.

He hears voices outside the bathroom.

"I don't want to go in."

"It's your mother."

"You don't have to tell me."

"It seems I do."

"I'll kill him."

"He had nothing to do with it."

"He had everything to do with it. Him and his scab buddies."

"He was just doing his job."

Patrick opens the door wide enough to see Dale, who's wearing dress pants, a white shirt and tie. His shoulders and forearms flex against the fabric. Sweat gleams on his forehead and the sides of his face. He tugs at the collar with a nail-bitten finger.

Belinda wears a cotton dress with an orange flower pattern and ruffled sleeves. The fabric clings to her breasts and hugs her hips. Orange earrings dangle from her ears. She adjusts Dale's tie.

"You look… handsome," she says with a smile.

She squeezes Dale's hand and pulls open the chapel door.

Wait for me, Patrick silently says, realizing he's not quite finished. *"Have you washed your hands?"* his mother would always ask whenever he came out of a public bathroom. He turns to the sink and his heart sinks. In the mirror he sees the wet stain in the crotch of his pants.

"Please God, please, not now, *ohhhhhh*…."

He rubs and rubs but pressing hard only makes things worse as the stain spreads. He balls up a wad of toilet paper and rubs it over his pants. It disintegrates, leaving white flecks. *"Mom."* He turns on the cold water, forms a cup with his hands, and allows the water to run. He holds his breath and presses his face into his hands. His lungs hurt. Slowly breathing out, he suddenly wonders if this is what his mother felt as she lay dying. Should he inhale the water and join her, leaving his grief behind? Would she greet him with open arms? Scold him for such impulsive foolishness? Tell him it will be all right? What is it like, he wonders, to breathe underwater?

=

Jenny greets Dale and Belinda with a pinched smile. Gently elbows Henry, who stares straight ahead, stone-faced. "Come on," Jenny begs. "For Maureen's sake."

Father and son eye each other. The vein in the middle of Dale's forehead pulses.

"Got some Wiser's wisdom in you?" Henry whispers through clenched teeth, referring to his son's newly acquired taste in whisky.

"Whatever it takes."

"At least he's here," Belinda adds.

"You too?" he asks, flicking the wrist in a sipping motion.

"Stop it," Jenny whispers. "Maureen's not two feet away from you and is this the best the two of you can do? Show a bit of respect, will you? That includes you," she says, giving Belinda a sharp once-over.

"You can't even make it to your mother's funeral without tipping the bottle. Disgraceful," Henry says.

"Just ignore him, hon," Belinda responds, stroking Dale's back.

"Have you no shame?"

"Have you no balls?"

"Your mother will turn in her grave."

"We're cremating her. Remember. In an *oak* coffin. What a waste of money."

"The details of your mother's funeral are none of your business."

"My mother is dead and Tanner and his white shirts—including you—wouldn't give us a ten-cent-an-hour raise. Ten fucking cents an hour."

"I'm just a foreman. So, don't damn well start blaming me. What's done is done. Got it?"

"What did I tell you two? This is not the time or the place to settle your differences," Jenny warns, her voice rising, red heat on her cheeks.

The door squeaks. His face red and a short lick of wet hair curled over one eye, Patrick stands in the doorway, one hand covering his crotch. Bits of toilet paper speckle his damp pantlegs. He makes a curt sad sound, feels the cool chapel air against his cheek.

"Oh my..." Jenny says, pressing her fingers against her mouth.

"Patrick..." Dale begins. Hey, buddy..."

"I'll, uh, get some towels," the attendant stammers, retreating through the door.

Patrick looks at them, his face calm. His father and brother hold his gaze. Suddenly he knows he will not be like them. He will join the navy and sail the seven seas. He will travel to the Arctic and live with Eskimos. Hitchhike to the Yukon and pan for gold. His house will have more than one bathroom and the wind will not whistle through cracked windows. He will drive a nice car. Marry a pretty girl.

Patrick will be warm, safe, loved.

# IN DEATH THERE IS LIFE (INSURANCE)

Bob Smithers sits in his car. He glances at his watch, knowing that the last thing the bereaved want is an insurance salesman who is late. He presses his tongue against his overbite. Bob is thinking of getting braces. He's still kicking himself for not taking advantage of his ex-wife's health care plan, which would have covered the procedure.

He stares at the cotton-coloured clouds that drift over the house. It is a sad-looking duplex with dented aluminum siding and windows in need of replacement. He loathes stepping into places like this, walking into living rooms that ooze of working-class struggle while the rawness of a lost one weighs heavy in the air.

He has to be careful with this one. This isn't just a mother dead from cancer or some father rear-ended by a drunk driver. Maureen Fitzpatrick was killed serving soup to striking workers at a local meatpacking plant, the irony being that the husband, Henry, was inside trying to keep the plant moving. The newspaper reported that the oldest son, Dale, was outside on the picket line when an arrow fell from the sky piercing the woman's heart. The good news — at least from Bob's perspective—is that the mother left behind two sons. *Mother of Dale and Patrick.* Bob figures they are ideal candidates for basic life policies and the trailing commissions that come with it—twenty percent off the top, declining to five percent for the duration of the policy. If he can convince the father to buy in as well, Bob stands to make a triple-shot sale.

Bob's motivation for getting braces is sex and money, his rationale being the better the smile, the better the chance with the former and more so with the latter. He is, however, conflicted. He knows that having railway tracks in his mouth will be money well spent. But at what cost? Dating, like sales, is competitive, and Bob needs every edge he can get. What woman would want to jump into the sack with overbite Bob? He's done a basic cost-benefit analysis of braces versus no braces. Has tried to get a sense of opportunities he'd missed with a full-blown metal mouth. Dental deficiency aside, Bob's had more than a few women tell him he's better than your average bear between the sheets. The question is, how many women will pass him over while his teeth are wrapped in chrome? Will he have to take special precautions during certain delicate situations?

He checks himself in the rear-view mirror. His sales training taught him that people make up their mind within ten seconds whether they want to continue. A stain on your tie? Zipper half down? A frown rather than a smile? Bits of lunch between your teeth? The sincerity of a handshake? It all comes into play when someone is deciding whether they want to do business with you. Or have sex with you.

Bob walks to the house like a Mormon on a mission. As he raises his knuckles to the door, Bob mutters his pre-sales mantra: *Always. Be. Closing.* With the sound of approaching feet inside, his predatory grin flips into a priestly smile.

Henry, his face white with grief, opens the door. Sorrow oozes out of every pore.

Bob extends a hand. "Mr. Fitzpatrick. Bob Smithers. We spoke on the phone. I am so sorry for your loss."

"Thank you."

"I'm here to help."

Bob breathes through his mouth as Henry leads him down the hallway. He senses the family's policy affordability as they make their way to the kitchen. The small things in the kitchen—the open peanut butter jar on the counter, the dishes in the sink— confirm that this is a house without a wife and mother. Bob lowers himself into a red vinyl chrome chair. Balls of white stuffing creep out of the edge of the arm rest. Henry sweeps crumbs off the table with his arm before collapsing into a chair across from him.

"My son, Patrick, he's upstairs. Dale, my oldest... I don't even know where he is. His girlfriend's, I suppose. We don't get along."

"Sorry to hear."

Bob runs his tongue over the top of his mouth as he prepares his first question, the answer to which he already knows.

"Your wife, Maureen. Did she have a will?"

"No real need for one. Least that's what we thought."

Bob slips a fingernail under Henry's scab of vulnerability and pulls. "You don't want things going into probate now, do you? You don't want to give them any more than you have to, do you?"

"Who?"

"The government."

Bob sees the anger building inside Henry—the image of jack-booted bureaucrats storming the house. It is the opening Bob is aiming for, the opportunity to reassure Henry that Bob will make things right. He reaches into his briefcase.

Bob spends the next hour outlining what needs to be done to bring closure to his wife's affairs. Each word, each sentence, is angled towards gaining Henry's confidence. The conversation eases towards the financial burden her death has brought to the family. Bob has a solution. Not now, he stresses. There are more important things to attend to.

"You're a good man," Henry tells Bob as he leads him to the front door.

=

Settling into his desk at the office, Bob ignores Richard Maxwell. Maxwell is a former Presbyterian minister who found his calling selling insurance rather than saving souls. Richard makes no bones about what he thinks of Bob's tactics. "There is a place in hell for ambulance chasers like you," he once told Bob.

"Behind every ambulance is some schmuck just trying to make a living," Bob replied, drawing a red circle around an obit he thought had potential.

Bob sits at his desk and mulls over his next move. There is always the unknown. With the Fitzpatricks, it will be with the son, Dale.

The two-week company training program Bob took when he started in the insurance game taught him that selling is a numbers game requiring thick skin, a deft touch, but above all, tenacity. A salesman needs to be thinking on his feet, continually strategizing to overcome obstacles that inevitably get in the way. A no is merely a yes looking for an opening. Bob's job is akin to a doctor probing your prostate—feel around long enough and you're bound to find something. Befriend with sincerity. Gain trust. Pay attention to the benign subtleties that make us human. Find an opening. Then go for the kill.

Over the years, Bob has honed his skills in duplicity and double-talk. He's the king of the hustle and proud of it. The slamming of a phone in his ear? A door closing in his face? Comes with the territory. He's been chased down and thrown out of almost every funeral home in the city. The result? He's had the highest closing ratio in the region two years running and regularly makes the President's Sales Circle Club. And he has the plaques to prove it.

Bob taps a pencil against a pad of paper. He stares at Richard. With two days until the end of the month, Richard and Bob are tied on the sales leader board. There is no way Bob's going to let Richard get the end-of-the-month sale bonus Keg gift card. All he needs to do is close the Fitzpatrick deal.

=

Henry opens the door, his eyes a dry sadness. As he beckons Bob in, Henry complains about the things he must attend to. He's been told that the best thing he can do is get the family back into their routine. Henry is mostly concerned about Patrick. He is supposed to return to school on Monday. Henry vents about the funeral home and the way they take advantage of the bereaved. The coffin. The flowers. The chauffeur-driven limousine. He had to throw it all on a credit card without having a clue how he will pay it off. Bob has been in the business long enough to know that buyer's remorse is part of the process. Henry has vowed to never be in a position of having to scrape up money for a funeral again. Which is why Henry has gathered Patrick and Dale into the living room.

Patrick sits in a worn chair in the living room, his knees pulled into his chest. He nods in Bob's direction. A red-eyed teenager sits on the edge of the couch, elbows on knees. He picks at the loose skin around a cuticle and stares at Bob. Over the phone, Henry warned Bob about Dale. "He won't be in any mood to sign anything. You can understand. He was there when it happened. He saw his mother die. Right before his eyes. He thinks it's all my fault. You understand?"

A square white bandage is taped to the side of Dale's head. It was just before Maureen's death, when striking workers tried to stop a bus full of scab workers from entering the plant, that Dale was clubbed by a cop.

"Dale, this is Mr. Smithers."

"Dale. Nice to meet you. How's your head?"

"What's it to you?" Dale growls back.

"If Mr. Smithers is good enough to take time out of his day to help us, the least you can do is show a little respect. Is that asking too much?" Henry asks, his eyes narrowing.

"I'm helping your father in his... in your... time of need," Bob says.

"You're just here to sell us some life insurance."

"I do not deny that I would like to sell you a life insurance policy. That's what I do for a living. Some people are plumbers. Others are artists. I sell insurance. Dale, you're what... eighteen?"

Dale nods.

"As much of a cliché as this is going to sound, why I'm here today is to try and give you, your brother here, and your father, peace of mind. Your mother would like that, wouldn't she? Peace of mind." He allows his words to settle in. "Her death is a tragedy and as God is my witness, I hope they find whoever did this."

"An arrow didn't kill my mother. Greed did."

"You might be right there," Bob responds with a sympathetic nod. "You know..." Bob continues, his eyes drifting towards

Patrick. "And Patrick also knows this as well…how your mother's death has caused your family a tremendous financial burden."

"We can deal with it."

"It's not anyone's fault."

"I said we'd deal with it."

"We will?" Henry cuts in. "How?"

"Your father and I have come up with an affordable plan that covers the three of you." He pauses, leaning forward to try to make eye contact. "Dale, this isn't glib. It's true. Life insurance is not for today. It's for tomorrow. It's for those we leave behind."

Dale lifts his head. He smirks. "Does it include dental care?"

Bob's stomach turns cold. He grits his teeth. Takes in a slow breath through his nose. He stares at Dale, holding back the urge to respond with something snarky to put this kid in his place. He reminds himself, twenty percent off the top. Five percent trailing. He smiles. "If you want to talk dental, we can talk about that some other time."

"What do you need me for anyway?"

"You're of age of consent. So, I need you to sign. Do you know what the number one cause of death of kids your age is?"

"Car accidents?"

"That's right. Look, Dale, I don't want to scare you into signing something you don't want to do. The question is, would you want the cost of a funeral to be placed on your father's back again?"

"Who's paying for this?"

"Initially. Your father."

Dale emits a small guffaw. "With what? Wooden nickels?"

"It's a small policy. Just enough to cover the basics. Maybe leave something extra for your dad and…" He pauses. "Your brother."

Dale glares at Henry. "She'd still be alive if it wasn't for him."

"That's not true. And you know it," Henry replies, his voice sharp.

"Maybe I should let the two of you work things out." Bob begins to rise. It's a familiar ploy. "We can always do this some other time."

Dale slides his eyes in Patrick's direction. "Does it matter who the beneficiary is?"

"If you assign the policy to Patrick and something should happen to you, things could get complicated. Proceeds would be held in trust until Patrick reaches the age of majority. Your father wouldn't be able to access the money for funeral expenses, which is why we're doing this in the first place."

"That's my deal."

"Think of your father."

"Oh, I'm thinking of him, all right."

Bob counts backward from ten. He hasn't come all this way, spent all this time, to let a commission slip through his fingers because of some smart-ass teenager. Okay, your mother died. People die every day. Get over it, you little shit. Bob presses his fingers into the arm of the chair. "Dale. Don't do this for your brother. Don't do it for yourself. Do it for your mother." He holds out a pen.

As the last light of the day tips behind the trees Bob walks to his car. He slips into the driver's door and closes the door. He sits, thinking, while he runs his tongue over the front of his teeth. Smacks his lips together. Presses his tongue against his overbite. Time to get braces.

# THE WORLD IS BUT A BROKEN HEART

Patrick Fitzpatrick walks down a snow-covered sidewalk knowing he shall soon be in the arms of a woman who can take away the cold. He checks the teachers' parking lot to ensure she hasn't left early.

They meet on Tuesdays and Thursdays, and when possible, on Saturdays. After classes end, he hangs around the school, careful not to stray near her homeroom or do anything that might draw attention. Sometimes he sees Mr. Carruthers looking at him from the end of a hallway, a glint of suspicion in his eyes. Saturdays are special. Candles are lit. Oysters and foreign-sounding cheeses offered, along with French bread. Music by Simone, Cohen, and Coltrane wafts through her small apartment. They talk and laugh. Laugh and talk. After they make love, Chantel will often ask him to read to her so she can improve her English. Later, she drops him off near his house, before his father, who cleans office buildings, arrives home for dinner.

The brake lights of her car burn yellow into the snow as Chantel slides to a stop. She pushes the passenger car door open. Her brown eyes beckon.

"Would you like a ride?" she asks. It is their joke, a well-rehearsed line between two actors in a play. As he slips in beside her, she meets him with a small peck that warms his face.

"Well?" she asks.

"Trigonometry," he groans.

"Never my best subject. But," she adds with an exaggerated sigh, "we will see. Eh?"

The car bores through thick flakes of snow. Classical music wafts over Patrick. The glow from the instrument panel illuminates Chantel's face.

After they park, an icy draft follows them through the glass front door of Chantel's building. Patrick blinks at the harsh light that floods the lobby as he waits for her to check her mailbox. She holds up a letter. It is from her fiancé, a medical student in Montreal. They plan to marry once she returns to Quebec. Inside the apartment, she fills the kettle for tea and hot chocolate, then sits and watches Patrick spread his homework out on the kitchen table.

"Pizza?" she asks.

=

The hissing of air brakes wakes Dale as the Greyhound pulls into the depot. He stares through the window at the tavern across the street. He disembarks, and drawn by the twang of meaningless country music, he hoists his duffel bag over his shoulders, and makes a beeline to the bar.

Near the entrance, he hears it, Kenny's laughter rising from the river valley. Ankle-deep snow fills his boots as he stumbles to the edge of the escarpment. He remembers peering down at a sliver of open water, jet black in the light of the full moon, his face blank with a thousand-yard stare. He runs his hands through his hair. He doesn't want to be here. Didn't want to come home. He has no other place to go.

Sitting on a barstool, his second beer half-drained, Dale peels back the label of the beer bottle. Two men in suits at a nearby table mull over their drinks. As Dale takes a sip, someone bumps him, pushing the lip of the bottle into his front tooth. He turns, ready to fight, beer foaming down his hand.

The young woman is wearing tight jeans and a T-shirt. "Oh my God," she says. "I didn't see you."

"It's okay."

She grabs a handful of paper napkins from the bar and attempts to wipe off the beer. "I'm sorry…"

Humiliation coils tight in Dale's chest as the two men smirk while the girl pats him down.

"You just getting into town?"

"Uh-huh."

"A lotta guys who work rigs come here to party when they get outta camp. You work rigs?"

"Uhuh."

The girl holds out her hand. "Jennifer."

"Thanks. I'm okay now."

She gets the message. Scampers away in a huff. Dale saunters down to the men.

"Howya doing?" inquires the older looking of the two.

"Something funny?" Dale asks.

"Did she just give you a nipple rub?" the younger one asks, guzzling back his beer.

"If some girl wants to pinch my nipple or suck on my dick, it's none of your business, now is it?"

The older man gives Dale a friendly salute. "Ten four, buddy." He motions to his companion. "Time to go."

"Don't listen to this rig-pig dipshit…"

Dale plows his fist into the younger one's face. Blood spurts from his nose. He manages a girlie slap across Dale's chin before he falls to the floor. Dale rams his elbow into the older man's gut. He grunts, clutches his ribs with one hand, holding up the other in surrender.

The bartender slams a baseball bat onto the bar. "Get the fuck outta my bar."

Dale saunters toward the front door, pausing to give Jennifer a wink, her eyes wide with fear and awe.

=

Chantel Baptiste is a small woman with high cheekbones and gleaming blue eyes. Almost nine years older than Patrick, her light-brown hair, cropped short, makes her look younger than twenty-four. The timbre of her voice and her sparkly disposition allow her to subdue even the most disruptive student. As she strolls the school's hallways, tribes of budding masculinity offer unsolicited waves. Some whisper crude catcalls about blowjobs and pussy, oblivious to the possibility that while she does not always hear or understand what they are saying, Chantel picks up from the tone of their voices and the thirst in their eyes the gist of their longing.

Chantel's duties include the supervision of an afternoon study hall in the cafeteria. The moment she arrives, students fixate on her like lemmings. Patrick is not her student. During study hall, she often shares stories of growing up in small-town Quebec where English is still rarely spoken and how she studied, first at Bishop's and then Université du Québec à Montréal, and how living in Montréal, combined with a year in France, opened her eyes. Until they became lovers, Patrick had no interest in French. Who needs French in a province where Texan is the unofficial second language and redneck the third?

Early in the school year, Susan Cripps, the English teacher who instructs her students with the authority of a prison matron, filled Chantel in about Patrick. "He's a lost soul. And who can fault him? His brother drowned three years ago. Then there's the strike. Picture this. The father's a foreman inside trying to keep the plant going. The oldest brother, Dale—he was a student here till he dropped out—he's out walking the picket line. The mother arrives to dole out soup to the strikers. In the blink of an eye, she's dead." She shook her head.

"Did they ever find him?"

"Who?"

"The one who did it?"

Susan shook her head. "That must gnaw on that poor kid, knowing that he could pass his mother's killer on the street and not even know it. Some days, he just sits in my class, staring out the window. And his father? He comes to parent-teacher interviews and just sits there." She gazes around the staff room. "All we're trying to do is make sure he gets through here in one piece. Give him enough of something to hang onto so he'll get by, be a labourer, maybe pick up a trade. Enough to settle down with a wife and kids. You know? That's what we all aim for, isn't it?" She sips her coffee.

Early in the school year, during study hall, Patrick had sat near the large cafeteria windows, far away from Chantel, textbook open but looking into the trees outside. After Halloween, moving from chair to chair, table to table, he slowly began to zigzag closer to Chantel. By the first week following Christmas break they found themselves alone, sitting at the same table. She felt him looking at the tan line that hugged the curve of her bra, which peeked out from her open-necked blouse. The line marked the point the tropical sun had failed to breach. His face went red as a coy smile crossed Chantel's face.

"I was in Cancun. With my boyfriend. Fiancé, now."

"Congratulations."

"He's going to be a doctor."

"He must be smart."

"He works hard."

"So, what are you doing here?" Patrick boldly says.

"I came to improve my English. And to try the dry cold." She giggles.

From then on, Patrick sat at Chantel's table. She eventually told him that she'd heard on the news about his mother's death while finishing her studies in Montreal. She supported the students' demands that Tanner products be banned from the university cafeteria. The next time they talked, Chantel offered to help Patrick with his homework outside of school hours.

=

They sit at her kitchen table befuddled by the sines and cosines that are supposed to make sense. "I will talk to Mr. Carlson." Carlson is the head of the school's math department, and one of several male teachers who have quietly offered to help Chantel with her English. Patrick laughed when she told him about Carlson inviting her for coffee after he lamented about his wife serving him divorce papers while gloating that she was sleeping with a man eight years her junior.

The lobby buzzer rings. Chantel rises.

"Pepperoni and…"

"A cab franc?" he guesses.

In addition to helping him with his homework, Chantel insists he learn the rudiments of wine. The way to a woman's heart, she tells him, includes a good wine. Patrick looks at her while they eat, his eyes full moons, the clock on the stove reminding him of the short time they have together.

"Come," Chantel whispers. She points to the bedroom.

Light from the streetlamp filters through sheers, casting an icy glow over the room. Chantel pulls her blue woollen sweater up her torso and toward the ceiling, pausing long enough to tease Patrick with her bronzed tummy, which rises and falls with the rhythm of her breathing. She flicks the sweater over her head, revealing breasts cupped by a black bra. This too falls to the floor. She locks her eyes on his as she wriggles out of her jeans.

"Your turn," she directs with a giggle.

Chantel helps Patrick out of his clothes until all that remains is a pair of worn white jockey shorts, tented with a youthful bulge. The air from the heating duct sends shivers down his spine. As she pushes him onto the bed, she pulls off his shorts. Chanel floats over him, her breasts swaying. She kneads her knees into the mattress and straddles him. Bites her lower lip as she pulls Patrick into her hips. Patrick sighs, flexes his stomach muscles as her weight presses into him. She leans forward and kisses him, her breath quick, shallow. A groan slips from deep within his throat.

They are lying side by side, Patrick bleached white by winter, Chantel browned by the Mexican sun. He gazes at the topography of her perfectly smooth skin, amazed at what she offers, self-conscious that he has little to give. She rests her head in the palm of her hand and stares at him. "It must be the Catholic in me."

"What do you mean?"

"This. Us. You. Your mother. Your brother."

"You had nothing to do with it. You were in Montreal."

"The first day I saw you, you had such a sad look on your face. Does what we do… this," she lifts her head and waves her hand. "Does it make you happy?"

"I don't know what happy is."

Chantel tells Patrick about living in Paris and of her brash and confident lover she had there, how he flaunted his American money and swagger, and above all, his passion. "He was—as we say in French—a *roué*."

"A *roué*?"

"Someone who devotes himself to sexual pleasure. He showed me there is nothing more passionate, more sensual, than a man making love to the woman he is with."

"Was he married?"

"When I asked him about being married, do you know what he said?"

"What?"

"That adultery is the purest form of happiness."

She pulls him into her and kisses his forehead.

"Someday you will understand."

She softly pats him on his back, then playfully pushes him away. "Time to get you home."

Chrysanthemum-sized snowflakes waltz around the car. Patrick sinks into the passenger seat, longing to spend every minute he can with Chantel, touching, talking to, and inhaling her. As she can him, he knows how to make her laugh, how to bring tears to her eyes. The more they are together, the more his need for her grows, for everything she imparts—the Eiffel Tower, the Champs-Élysée, the anonymity she found in great cities, and conveniently, the reluctance she secretly felt when she accepted her fiancé's marriage proposal. She responded with a quiet sympathy when he told of the aftermath of Kenny's drowning and how Dale turned to drugs and alcohol, the enmity between Dale and Henry on opposite sides of the picket line, and how an arrow falling from the sky pierced his mother's heart.

As they near his street, Patrick silently prays that Chantel will turn the car around, take him to her apartment where they will spend the night together, wake to the sun tilting through her windows. They will share breakfast, make love again, and go to school satiated.

"Are you all right?" she asks.

"Yes," he says quietly. "You make me happy."

"It has to be a careful happy."

"But who will know?"

"That's the thing. We have to make sure that nobody knows. Ever. Okay?"

"Okay."

"Remember, I am a teacher first. A lover second."

Patrick gets out of the car and as Chantel pulls away, she stares at him in the rear-view mirror, knowing it is not so much a line she has crossed, but an unspeakable void she's entered, one that a teacher or any adult is meant to disturb. She makes the sign of the cross, signals left, turns, and drives, sensing regret swoop into the pit of her stomach, wondering if, in some small way, she has done more harm than good. Yet, when they're together, whether in study hall or at her apartment, she sees—what nobody else can—this boy who has suffered so much suddenly come to life.

Patrick stares at the pickup truck rusting in the driveway. It is a beater. But it is his beater. His father gave it to him for Christmas. He will be sixteen in July, plans to get his licence, and wants to take a body-shop class in the fall. Buy a set of chrome rims. Maybe paint the truck canary yellow.

Dale is splayed out on the couch, an empty beer can on his chest. "What's up?" he asks, rising, catching the can before it falls to the floor.

"Where's your truck?"

"Welcome home to you, too, buddy." Dale gives Patrick an awkward hug.

"What happened to your face?"

"Smacked it on the bathroom wall of the bus."

"You took the bus?"

"I lost my truck in a poker game. It needed work anyway. So I said fuck it and grabbed a Greyhound." Dale crushes the can in his hand and strolls into the kitchen. "Want one? Wouldn't go over very well with the old man, now would it? Why don't you see if there's a game on? I'll make us something to eat."

"How long you here for?"

"Till the old man kicks me out. Least till spring breakup's over. Government pulls rigs offa the roads this time of year otherwise they chew the shit outta the asphalt." He pulls a fresh beer from the refrigerator. "Hell, I might not go back at all. I got enough hours to collect pogey. I might just go out and party till I puke. How's school?"

"It's okay."

"You gonna pass?"

"Maybe."

"I hated school. Hated the teachers. Principal was a goofball. Was glad to get the hell outta there. But you, you kinda like that shit."

"Not really."

"I can probably get you on as a swamper in the summer. The work sucks but the paycheques are three-figures clean." Dale pulls on his beer tab. Phsst. "So, how is he?"

"Same old. Same old."

Dale forms a line with his thumb and forefinger. "Henry Fitzpatrick cleaned six thousand two hundred and forty-seven toilets in his life. *Fuuuck*."

"He's doing the best he can."


Patrick drifts upstairs to his room. He lies on his bed, desperate to call her. Chantel refuses to give him her telephone number, lest it fall into the wrong hands. He pulls a pillow over his face and closes his eyes. The image of his mother sends his heart reeling. Panic seizes him. What would she say if she knew about *her*? Would she flip out, scream, call the school? The police? But his mother is no longer here. He opens his eyes. Breathes. He thinks of the first time he saw Chantel naked. How when they kissed, their teeth knocked together, and they giggled. He glows, retracing how she guided his every move, careful to temper his growing excitement. "*Voulez-vous coucher avec moi*?" he whispers to himself, cringing at the hackneyed French he had attempted to use as foreplay during their first afternoon together.

"Very good," she'd laughed. "I must teach you."

"Why me?" he asked later. "Why not Gordon Baxter?"

Baxter is a provincially ranked track-and-field star. Patrick is a spare on the football team.

"Because," Chantel said, tapping his forehead with her index finger. "You have something he will never have." Her brow curled into a furrow.

"After my mother died… Yes," she said, responding to his gaze. "When I was your age, I was a bit of what you say…a wild child. I hung around, drinking…partying…and yes, having sex with my boyfriend. One day, my teacher, Ms. Douchette, she said to me, 'Chantel, you have a choice. You can stay in Rimouski, find a job or marry a nice boy who works in the mill. Or…'" Chantel pointed through the window, "'…you can look at the moon and dream.'" She kissed Patrick's hand. "You can do more than work with your hands. Not," she continued with a wink, "that there is anything wrong with your hands."

=

The sound of the front door opening and closing, followed by a pair of boots hitting the floor, wakes Patrick. Henry growls as he shuffles from the hallway to the living room. Patrick opens his bedroom door and listens.

"You know the rules. No freeloading. Rent's due at the beginning of the month. Got it?"

"Good to see you too," Dale replies, his voice unfriendly.

Patrick stops partway down the stairs. Dale and Henry are watching hockey on the television. Still in his work clothes, Henry sits in his threadbare man-chair, a permanent scowl on his face, his hand firmly on a can of his own brand of cheap beer. Dale is on the couch, cradling his own beer, his eyes darting between the television and the truck outside the living-room window.

"I told Patrick about losing my truck."

"That so."

"I need something to get around."

"How 'bout if you just let me watch the game."

"What about the truck out front?"

"It's your brother's."

"He doesn't have a licence."

"What's that got to do with the price of milk?"

Dale sees Patrick standing at the base of the stairs. "Mind if I use your truck? Just till I get some wheels of my own."

"I don't even know if it'll start."

"Where're you gonna get the money for gas?" Henry asks, his eyes glued to the game.

"I got cash."

"For rent?"

"I'll get you your rent money."

"Good. It's already late."

"Hey, Paddy. I'll put insurance on it. Promise."

"Will you teach me to drive?"

Henry belches. "You can't teach someone to drive a three on the tree with a spring clutch in the city."

"How's he gonna learn then?"

"Once the snow's gone, I'll take him for a ride outside the city. Now, can I watch the game?"

Patrick looks at his brother. "If I let you use the truck, will you take me to see Mom?"

Dale pauses, reluctance in his eyes. "Sure."

=

Winter passes. The first robins and warblers of the year appear. The Saturday sun, yolk-yellow in the blue and white sky, warms Chantel and Patrick as they sip hot chocolate, sitting on a log near the riverbank. She had asked him to take her into his world, down to the river valley where he used to hang out with Dale and Kenny. At his request on the way there, they took a detour to the meat plant, now closed, where his mother had died, pulling up alongside the chain-link fence that surrounds the brick building. "Right there," was all Patrick could say while pointing to the spot where Maureen had fallen. He dropped his right hand to his lap and stared out the windshield, Chantel's hand on his shoulder. Without a word, they continued east on Jasper Avenue before parking and on foot headed down to where the fort used to be on the riverbank before last year's flood swept it away.

"We'd put branches over the tarps so that the city wouldn't think it was a place for homies and bums and tear it down. When my father got drunk and stupid, or stupid and drunk, we'd come down here and freeze our asses off until we figured he'd passed out. Fuck, it was fun."

"Patrick…"

"Sorry…" He stares out at the river. "Kenny loved it down here. Winter. Summer. Didn't matter. He'd come home with all kinds of bugs, dead animals. It used to gross our mother out. He said that when he grew up he wanted to work for Parks Canada— you know, ride the range, rescue people, track bears, teach kids about nature." He pauses. "Then he died." He gestures to a fallen black spruce tree that arches over the water. "He fell off that branch and through the ice."

"Your brother, Dale. He was there?"

Patrick nods.

"The old man had gone ape-shit on Kenny, so Dale brought him down here till things settled down."

They sit in silence, wind mixed with traffic sounds filtering down from the street above, whispering through the trees.

"He's still out there, you know."

"Who?"

"Kenny. I saw him." Patrick nods toward the middle of the river.

"When?"

"Two winters ago. My father and Dale were fighting. For sure I thought Dale was going to clock him. As usual, my mother was stuck in the middle. Dale had just quit school—he'd been failing anyway —and my father wanted to kick him out. With all three of them yelling and screaming, I said fu… firetruck it. Have you ever seen the northern lights?"

"Not until I came to Edmonton."

"I was lying on my back in the snow, a thirteen-year-old kid drinking his first rye whiskey, staring at the northern lights. And then I saw him. Laughing and running. Kenny had this big grin on his face. Then you know what he did?" Patrick beckoned with his middle finger. "He wanted me to join him. Come out onto the ice." He looks at Chantel, his eyes brimming. "The next thing I know, Dale's shaking me awake. I woulda froze to death if he hadn't found me."

"Did you ever tell anyone? About seeing Kenny?"

"I couldn't tell my father. My mom, if I'd told her, she'd a come down here looking for him."

"Your poor mother. Your poor brother."

"Which one?"

"Both." Chantel puts her hot chocolate down on the log and pulls Patrick into her. "You still have them, you know. Kenny. Your mom." She presses a finger to her temple. "Up here." She puts her hand over her heart. "And here." She pulls him to his feet. "Come."

The next Wednesday, when Patrick leaves school at four o'clock, he hears, then sees, the truck. The engine growls loudly before groaning into a noisy rumble. Dale waves him over.

"Climb in."

"Where're we going?"

"Where do you think?"

They stand at the foot of their mother's grave. Patrick holds a bouquet of flowers they picked up at a nearby convenience store, uncertain what to do with them. Dale walks over to an adjoining grave.

"What they don't know won't hurt them," he says, smirking as he takes a metal flower holder and plants it in front of their mother's flat headstone. "Love you," he says to the rectangular grey granite before straightening up and turning toward the truck. He gives Patrick a wink. "Cemeteries give me the heebie-jeebies."

Dale slinks into the driver's seat, pulls a mickey from his jacket, and takes a pull, his eyes keyed on Patrick.

"What'd ya say?" Dale flips the bottle into a pocket when Patrick opens the passenger door and climbs in.

"I told her that I missed her."

"That's what I said too. But more in a…" he puckers his lips into a squirrely grin, "…uh, you know, telepathic sort of way. Did you tell her I'm teaching you how to drive?"

Patrick's face lights up. "What about..."

"What he don't know won't hurt him."

Patrick leans over the steering wheel, his gloved hands damp.

"I don't know why he bought you this pile of shit anyway," Dale says, affectionately patting the dashboard. "Arm-strong steering... three on the tree... clutch with a kick." Dale gestures with his hands as he speaks. "Make sure it's in neutral." He reaches across and tests the shift for play. "Nice 'n' easy. 'Kay? So, clutch in."

"I know..."

"Find first. Good. Ease out the clutch. Ease in the gas. Clutch back in. Shift down to second. Clutch up. Gas down. Up and over into third. Got it?"

"'Course."

"No, ya don't. No one gets it right the first time. Especially when it's a three on the tree." Dale scans the empty cemetery. "Want to give it a go?" He laughs. "The most we can do is end up like everyone else in this place."

Patrick turns the key. Pops the clutch. The truck lurches forward. Stalls. Dale resists the urge to smile. Patrick grits his teeth, straightens his left leg as he forces the clutch into the floor. Turns the ignition. The engine stutters to life.

"Good. Ease out the clutch... Feather the gas." The truck inches forward. "Straight into second." Dale winks. "Slow and easy. Patrick drops into second. The truck picks up speed as he finds third.

"That's it."

They crest a small incline.

"Careful. Watch where you're going..."

"What do you think I'm doing?"

"Slow it down..." Dale leans forward in his seat, his voice short. "Gear down. I said... gear down..."

The engine revs as the gears grind. The truck slides, lurches left. Patrick panics. Jams on the brakes. The truck stalls inches from a turn-of-the-century marble angel marker. Patrick blinks. Exhales. Wipes his brow. Dale snorts out a "wa-hoooo...," high-fiving Patrick and chuckling as his younger brother sweats bullets while grinning as if he'd just gotten away with something illegal. Their smiles turn into laughter, something they haven't shared in years.

Dale and Patrick sit slumped over the kitchen table. Standing at the kitchen counter, Henry runs a hand through his nest of greying hair, then thrusts a finger at Dale. "You let him drive?"

"Get that finger outta my face."

This is all Patrick's fault. And Patrick knows it. He'd rushed through the front door, his mistake being the second he gushed out to Henry that he now knew how to drive a standard.

"With no licence?" Henry yelled.

"We were in the cemetery," Dale replied with a shrug.

"What kind of imbecile are you anyway?"

"The kind that came from the same gene pool as you."

Henry slams a fist on the counter. He steps toward his oldest son, towers over him, pokes his middle finger into his forehead. "You got rent money?"

Dale whips out his wallet and tosses a wad of bills at his father, which flutter to the floor. "There. Happy?"

"I'll be happy the day you move out."

Dale pushes his chair back and rises, his right fist clenched and ready. They eye each other, a game of chicken to see who will pull the first punch. Henry turns, presses his hips into the stove, head between his hands.

"I regret the day you were born..." he says, his voice paper-thin.

Dale storms out the door.

=

The afternoon Saturday sun streams through Chantel's bedroom window. "Mr. Carruthers was asking about you," she says as they lie in bed. "He says your teachers have seen an improvement in your studies and," giving his nose a tweak, "your attitude."

"Really?"

"I said that all I do is supervise the study hall. He'd also heard that I had asked Mr. Carlson about math."

"You did?"

"Most certainly. I explained that I'd told Mr. Carlson you were going to get through trigonometry come hell or high water." She laughs at her choice of words.

"What did Carlson say?"

"He wished me luck."

"Fucker."

"Patrick," she says, sternly. "If you don't pass trigonometry, you'll have to repeat. Then you'll be behind."

"It's not like I have any use for trig."

"But you do want to graduate? Right?"

"What if I come to Montreal?"

"Don't be silly."

Patrick pouts.

Chantel smiles, touched by his reaction. "Someday you will meet someone. You will have a wonderful life. A happy life. Come. Let's get you home."

An aloofness descends over Chantel's face as she drives. She glances at Patrick. He returns the look of a wounded bird.

"It's okay if we get caught, you know."

"No, it isn't."

"Nobody will know. Promise."

She pulls the car to the curb at the usual spot. "I could lose my teacher's licence." She leans over. "I'm the big bad wolf and you're an innocent lamb. *Grr*…"

He pulls on the door handle, hoping she will say something more. She blows him a kiss. "What are the consequences of a happy life, eh?"


Patrick walks down the street, and nearing his house, hears the truck. It fishtails around the corner and barrels past. Patrick watches, dumbstruck. Brake lights blink as it knifes between two parked cars, coming to a stop inches from the front steps. Looking over his shoulder, Patrick begins to run, half-expecting to see a convoy of police cruisers storm around the corner. He whips open the driver's door. "Dale, Dale. Come on. Get up. Before the cops come." He yanks on Dale's jacket. Slips on the ice.

"*Fuuuuck…* Hey, Paddy. Whatcha doing?"

"Get outta the truck."

"Story of my life." He rolls his head round and round and sings. "Fucked up once... Fucked up twice... Holy fucking Jesus Christ," before flopping out of the driver's seat to the icy ground and onto his stomach. "*Fuuuck*," he yelps.

"Hurt my hand."

Rolling onto his back, he props himself against the truck's front tire. "You know, bro, I've had it with women. Just had it." Leans his head against the tire. "You know what my problem is? I like women. Pure and simple. Love 'em to bits." He presses the knuckles of his good hand into the snow and forces himself to his feet. Sways back and forth, fighting to remain standing. "How's this?"

"Get in the house."

"I'm pretty hammered. The ol' man's sure gonna be pissed. Well, he can go fuck himself."

Dale lets Patrick pull him into the house. Drops onto the couch.

Patrick races back outside and jumps into the driver's seat. With desperate turns of the key, he sparks the engine to life. Shakes with fear, cautiously backs onto the street. Chugs the truck toward an open spot. Grinds it into reverse and attempts to parallel park. Stalls. Bangs the steering wheel with his fists. "Fuck. Fuck. Fuck." Mutters. *Neutral. Neutral. Clutch in. Reverse. Ease the clutch out— stiff but gentle.* As he eases the truck back along the curb, a cruiser, lights flashing, turns the corner and pulls up alongside.

A policeman steps out of the cop car and motions to Patrick to roll down his window. "This your truck?"

"Sort of... Yes."

"You can't sort of own a truck. Licence and registration."

"I don't have my licence. Yet. Sir."

"You don't?"

"I was trying to park."

"Without a licence?"

"My brother accidentally drove it onto our front yard."

The policeman sees the tracks embedded into the snow-covered lawn for the first time. He looks at the truck, which appears more abandoned than parked.

"How does one accidentally drive a truck onto a front lawn?"

"'Cause he...had to throw up. He's got...leukemia."

"Leukemia?" The policeman repeats. "Does he know you took his truck?"

"It's not his truck. It's mine. I lent it to him."

"You own the truck. But you don't have a licence."

"Uhuh."

"Give me the keys."

Henry drives up, jumps from his car, and comes running. "What the hell…"

"This your son?"

"What's it to you?"

"Sir, we can make this hard."

Henry calms down. "Sorry…"

The officer thumbs a gloved hand at Patrick.

"Driving without a licence. How old's the one with leukemia?"

"Leukemia?" Henry stares at Patrick, his eyes wide.

"He was coming home from his girlfriend's. Thought he was going to throw up." Patrick nods. Looks over at his father. "Like he did before? Remember?"

"Where'd he throw up?" the officer asks. "Not that I need to know."

"It's uh… pretty, you know—chunky…"

The policeman gives Patrick one last stare-down. "I get the picture." He shakes his head. "Terrible way to go." Nodding in the direction of the truck, he hands Henry the keys. "Get it off the street." He tips a finger towards Patrick. "And take care of that brother of yours."

He slips into his cruiser and pulls away.

"Leukemia?" Henry shakes his head. He looks at Patrick, suddenly serious. "Did your brother tell you what happened to his truck?"

"He lost it in a poker game."

"Bullshit. He broke his boss's jaw. Handed the registration over to him so he wouldn't have him charged with assault." Henry tosses Patrick the keys. "See if you can park this thing."

Patrick hears the yelling before he gets into the house. Dale is slack-jawed on the couch. Henry kicks the coffee table aside and pulls him to his feet. "You drunk lazy fuck."

Dale takes a blind swing at Henry. Misses. Henry wheezes with effort as he hits Dale with a blow to the ribs. Dale flinches. Cinches Henry into a bear hug. Henry knees him in the groin. His body suddenly void of structure, he falls.

"Come into my house...eat my food..." Winding back to drill Dale, Henry catches Patrick flush on the side of the face. As Patrick reels backwards into the kitchen, Dale rolls onto his hands and knees, sucks in what air he can, pushes himself up with his good hand, and launches into Henry, knocking them both onto the floor, Dale on top. As he readies a haymaker, a frying pan slams across his forearm.

"Get offa him!" Patrick looms over Dale, holding the frying pan with both hands.

"You broke my wrist."

"It's not all I'm gonna break. Now get off."

Dale flops onto the floor next to Henry. Side by side they lie, eyes closed, too exhausted to move. All is quiet except for their breathing. Dale lets out a long chuckle. "Ah fuck. Like father, like fucking son. Eh?" He strikes his head on the floor and passes out.

Patrick tosses the frying pan onto the couch. Curses as he steps over them. Grabs his jacket and flies out the front door.

Chantel, leaning against the wall, closes her eyes and presses the buzzer with the sudden realization she's gotten more than she bargained for.

"Oh, *pauvre petit*," she says as she opens the door to her apartment.

Patrick snorts back a thick stream of snot. "I got in the way of a knuckle sandwich," he says with a false hint of bravado. "See." He runs a finger over the welt in his cheek before crumpling into tears and pressing his face against her shoulder.

Chantel guides him to the kitchen table and gently sets him down. Sitting in the chair opposite, she clasps his frozen fingers with one hand while rubbing the palm of the other over his shoulder till the sobs subside.

"It doesn't matter. In June, I'm sixteen," he huffs, his eyes red. "I can do whatever I want and he won't be able to do a thing about it."

"Let's clean you up. Have you got somewhere to stay? A friend."

He shakes his head. "I have no friends."

"You need to call your father. Tell him you are staying with a friend. That way, he won't worry."

After warming Patrick up with a cup of hot tea and listening as he makes excuses with Henry, Chantel guides him to the bedroom, where out the window they observe a homeless man push a grocery cart down the sidewalk. He salutes them with a mittened thumbs-up. Chantel coils her arms around Patrick. They lie on her bed listening to the silence they inhabit. The last thing he sees as he falls asleep is Chantel watching the rise and fall of his chest.

The next morning, as they near the school, Chantel pulls the car into a strip mall. "You should walk from here," she instructs, her voice firm. Patrick opens the door but remains sitting. He stares at her, feeling needy but not sure exactly what it is that he needs.

"Can I..."

"Patrick. Please, just get out of the car."

As he attempts to give her a kiss on the cheek Chantel glances through the driver-side window. Chuck Carlson. Waiting on a red light. He gives her the *gotcha* smile he shoots at students when he catches them cheating on a test. Patrick sees the colour drain from Chantel's face.

"What?"

At the end of the day Chantel is gathering her materials when Carlson strides through her classroom door. "Do you have a minute?" He places his left foot on the seat of the desk directly in front of hers, leans forward, cups his chin in the palm of his hand, and rubs his index finger along his jaw. "Not good," he says, shaking his head. "Not good at all."

"Not good what?"

"I saw you."

"It was…"

"Innocent? It always is until you're caught."

"Patrick was cold."

"He's not the only student who walks to school. I don't know of any other student who gets a ride with his study teacher—complete with a kiss."

"I'm not his teacher."

"You could very well be. It's rather unusual, wouldn't you say, a teacher giving a lonely student a ride to school?" He rounds the desk, presses his buttocks into the desktop, sits, and crosses his arms over his chest. "Teachers have been talking about you. Did you know that?" His voice turns sinister. "You could lose your licence. This will follow you wherever you go. Even to Quebec."

"For what?"

"Really," he responds, dubious.

"It was nothing."

"Then you don't mind if I talk to Mister Carruthers."

"We were talking."

"About?"

"School. Things." Chantel sighs. "Hasn't Patrick been through enough?"

"You think you're special, don't you? Think this doesn't happen all the time? Students falling in love with teachers? That's why we pay union dues. So it can all be swept under the carpet to protect horny teachers' little asses. The big difference here is that *I saw you*. He lets his words sink in. "Tell you what, though. I'll make you a deal." He laughs. "*Vivre Sa Vie.*"

"*Vivre sa vie?*"

"French New Wave. Jean-Luc Godard. Nineteen sixty-two. It's playing at the Princess Theatre on Saturday. Why don't you meet me there?" Before she can respond, he thoughtfully presses a finger against his lips. "I'll even buy the popcorn." He winks, steps toward the door, turns on a heel, and smiles. "You're fortunate."

"*Pourquoi?*"

"The age of consent in Alberta is fourteen."

=

Henry picks up the phone and dials Sheila's number. Soon after he started working at Tanner Meats, he allowed himself a brief fling. Sheila was a secretary at the plant and he would often chat her up when he had personnel matters to deal with. From the beginning, he knew she was the type of woman men wanted to jump into bed with. One day, out of the blue, she told Henry that she and her husband had split up after he'd caught her with a Haitian line worker. "I was bored to tears in my marriage," she said, matter of factly. "Missionary poistion is for Mormons and morons. What about you?"

"I'm a happily married man," he replied.

"You know there's a rule about 'happy' and 'married' not being used in the same sentence?" Sheila blew her cynicism into the air on a wisp of cigarette smoke.

The first time they got together, Sheila made it clear this was no more than a one-off- after-work-fuck-n-fly. Nothing as serious as love would follow him. Less than five minutes after Henry stepped through the door to her apartment, they were naked on the living-room floor, pumping away. It was all no-holds-barred, selfish sex. She told him that the prospect of his grinding masculinity excited her. She screamed things Henry had only heard watching porn movies at stag parties when he was young. He didn't know what to make of her but obediently continued to grind away, thinking this was what it was like to be with a nymphomaniac. The routine was always the same. Fuck. Dress. Leave. Repeat. The only thing that changed was the sexual position she demanded on any particular day.

Then one evening Henry knocked on the door, and she didn't answer.

"Variety is the spice of life, right?" Sheila said when they met then next day in the plant parking lot. "Besides, I don't want any foolhardy adult stupidity to affect your kids. Too many divorces as it is." Besides, she admitted to having someone new on her radar.

They got in their cars and drove off in separate directions. Henry was relieved. Maureen couldn't make nohow of Henry when he gave her a rare quick hug after he got home.

When Patrick comes through the door, Henry scowls at him, his hands immersed in dishwater. "Where were you?"

Patrick blinks, searching for a response. "Around."

"Around where?"

"What are you doing home so early?"

He tosses a fork back into the water. "We lost the cleaning contract on a building. They're cutting back my hours."

This comes as no surprise to Patrick. It's just the way his father's life has gone. If he could rename him, he'd call his father "Never Enough Fitzpatrick." What Patrick realizes as he stares at him is how much he hates this failure of a man standing over the sink in his matching dark blue Bee-Clean pants and shirt. The nail of Henry's left big toe sticks out of a dirty tube sock. He smells of cleaning agents, a half-empty pack of smokes pressing out of a shirt pocket embroidered with a smiling bee pushing a vacuum cleaner.

"If Mom was around…"

"Well, she's not," Henry replies curtly, working a fingernail under a piece of dried food before tossing the plate back in.

"She'd still be alive if you hadn't taken the foreman's job."

"That so?"

"She told you not to take it. Not to be a shirt."

"I did what was best. For her. For you. For all of us. I needed to put food on the table…keep us going… I needed…" Henry presses the palm of his hands into the sink. Rests his forehead on the water tap. His voice is barely a mumble. "I'm sorry. Just plain sorry."

Patrick would like nothing better than to grind his knuckles into his father's kidneys, make him pee blood like he'd seen in *Raging Bull* and *Rocky*. "We're so past sorry."

Henry straightens, dropping his hands to his sides. "I just hope you and your brother do a helluva lot better than I ever did."

"That's a pretty low bar."

Patrick turns and flees up the stairs, slamming his bedroom door behind him.

Henry dries his hands, drops the damp dish towel, and with his foot wipes up the water that has dripped onto the floor. He throws it onto the counter, walks to the front door, and yanks his coat from the closet. Stares up the stairs. "Go ahead. Be like your brother. Drop out of school. Be a swamper. See if I care. You may not want me to be your father, but I'm still your legal guardian."

From his bedroom window, Patrick watches Henry back his Eldorado, which he'd bought as a reward for moving into management at the plant, out of the driveway and pull away.

The full moon casts a dead grey-white paste on the plant. Henry sits in the driver's seat staring at the broken windows, the killing chute, the waiting pens, the frozen mud and cow shit layered with dirty snow, until his eyes drift to where Maureen died. He pulls out a bottle. Unscrews the cap. Before the liquor can reach his tongue, he lays his head against the steering wheel and weeps. Tears fall from his face to his jeans. Henry gathers himself. He stares at the sky, star-scattered, gauzy with moonlight. He steps out of the car, screams at the top of his lungs, and hurls the bottle against the building.

Patrick buzzes Chantel's apartment at the usual time on Saturday, but she does not answer. He presses the buzzer again, and again.

Patrick exits the foyer, steps back and stares up at the apartment. The drapes are drawn. The lights off. Patrick trudges to a nearby corner coffee shop where he downs a hot chocolate and a doughnut before returning to her building. He follows a tenant through the locked foyer door and takes the steps to the third floor two at a time.

"Chantel, I know you're in there," he whispers into the door. He steps back, raises his voice, and begs. "Please." A woman down the hall opens her door and answers his plea with a suspicious look. Patrick turns and leaves.

Teeth pressed together, Chantel sits in a movie seat with a bag of popcorn in her lap, eyes focused on the screen as tears fall from Anna Karina's fawning eyes in a sixties black-and-white Paris. Her hand clutches the armrest that separates Chuck Carlson from her. It is her own fault she has to sit through this. She let her guard down. Gave him the opportunity to hold over her what he saw. Since she was a young girl, she's known that all it takes is a touch, a look, to give a boy, a man, what he wants so she can get what she wants. She studies Carlson out of the corner of her eye. Squirms in her seat as he skims a finger over Chantel's hand before reaching for the popcorn. She responds by digging into the popcorn bag first, wiping the butter from her fingers on the seat beside her.

As they leave the theatre, Chantel stares up into the flakes of spring snow falling through the yellow light that the marquee casts onto the sidewalk. He asks her what she thought of the film. She has no real view on the French New Wave, having grown up immersed in the films of Quebec directors like Claude Jutra and Denys Arcand. A glacial quiet follows.

Carlson takes a deep gulp of cold air and turns to her. "Do you have any wine?"

Chantel's Toyota is missing from the parking lot when Patrick arrives at school on Monday. He peers through the window of her homeroom. It's empty. Maybe she's in the teachers' room, he thinks. Between classes, he passes her room again and again, hoping to catch a glimpse of her. A substitute teacher peers up from Chantel's desk. Rumours spread. Ms. Baptiste has resigned. Been fired. Headed back to Quebec. She has cancer. At lunchtime, Patrick sees Carlson coming out of his classroom. They stare each other down.

"Patrick?"

"What?"

"She's gone home."

"What do you mean?"

"Something about her mother being sick."

Patrick rushes to his locker, grabs his jacket, sprints to the school office, and tells the secretary that he has a dentist appointment. As he signs out, he senses someone watching him. Carlson is standing outside the large office window. He gives Patrick a wink and continues on.

Chantel opens the apartment door. She stares at Patrick, her eyes a mix of anger and concern. "You mustn't be here." Patrick does not move. He cannot move. He looks at her, his head bent at the neck, his mouth stiff from the cold. He wets his upper lip with his tongue and closes his mouth, unable to say a word.

Chantel leads him through the door. "You need to warm up." She wraps her arms around him.

Two suitcases are open on the living room floor.

"It's true, isn't it? You're leaving."

"Yes, I'm going home to Montreal. My mother. She is sick."

"But you told me your mother is dead."

"She is. But I had to find a reason. Nobody here but you knows about her death." She stares at him. "I cannot risk staying. People know."

"Who?"

"Mr. Carlson."

"Carlson. What the fu…"

"Don't. Please."

"How?"

"Does it matter?"

She leads him into the living room and waits as he sheds his jacket. They step over the suitcases and onto the couch. Chantel rests her elbows on her knees. Her hands dip and doodle, dance as if she wants to let them do the talking. "Patrick," she says. She hooks her thumbs under her chin. "You have friends at school. People who want to help you. People who want to see you graduate."

"Like who?"

"Mr. Carruthers."

"Carruthers?"

"He has a soft spot for you. I can tell. He wants you to be safe. Like me, he wants you to make something of yourself."

"But what about you? Us."

"I'll go back to Montreal and apply to teach in the fall. No questions asked. This was an exchange with a teacher who lives in this apartment. Not a permanent teaching position."

Her eyes trap him with a look so intense he cannot move. She dabs the side of her eyes with the heel of her hand.

"What's the world without a broken heart, eh?"

Chantel pulls the car over at the usual spot. A dusting of snow falls. After a few silent minutes, she turns to Patrick and cups his cheeks with her hands. "If you remember nothing else, remember this. You don't belong to your brother. You don't belong to your father. And, God rest her soul, you don't even belong to your mother. You belong to *je ne sais quoi*." She kisses him on the cheek. Her eyes remain locked on Patrick as he opens the door and slips out.

Patrick ignores the truck, dead in the driveway, as he unlocks the front door. The house is dark except for the white fluorescence of the stovetop light. Breakfast dishes, smeared with soggy flakes of cereal, breadcrumbs, and strawberry jam, sit in the sink while the previous night's dinner dishes are stacked in the drying rack. His mother would scream to high heaven if she saw her kitchen in such a mess. He stares at the dishes, resisting the urge to wash and dry them and put them away. Clean up your own goddamn dishes, he mutters, before flopping onto the living-room couch. Just as quickly, he bounces back up and heads to the door.

Chantel turns down Patrick's street. She's never seen his house. Recognizes it only by his description of the truck. She doesn't even know why she has come, only that she must. What she will say she can't imagine. Teachers are not in the habit of making house calls. Certainly not to say goodbye. The house is dark. She waits, hoping a light will come on or that he will show up on the street. Her car's antenna quivers in the wind. Late snow continues to fall. Chantel pulls away and drives up and down the nearby neighbourhood streets. She slows to peer through the windows of convenience stores, going as far as the school before turning back. This time there's a light on in the living room. She cuts the engine, listens to the ticking sound of it cooling. She steps out of the car and silently prays that Patrick will be alone.

Dale answers the door.

"I'm Chantel Baptiste, Patrick's study hall supervisor."

He looks at her dubiously. "Isn't he a lucky duck?"

"I need to talk to him."

"He's not here."

"Do you know where he might be?"

"I'm his brother. Not his babysitter."

"I have to return home to Montreal and want to give him some books I thought he would like to read." She looks at Dale. "Would he have gone down to the river? To the fort?"

"What do you know about the fort?"

"Patrick may have told me things he shouldn't have. We went for a walk one Saturday."

"You went for a…"

"He showed me where your brother fell through the ice."

The sky is losing the sun as Dale and Chantel stumble through the opening in the brush that leads to the log she and Patrick had shared weeks before. A half-empty mickey sits on top of the log. Chantel scans the river ice, gasps, her eyes riveted on a small speck. Dale follows her gaze. Momentarily frozen at the sight of his brother so far out, so close to open water, he rushes down the riverbank. Holding the branch of a tree, he puts one foot on the ice. Tests it. He lets go of the branch, takes a second step, and the ice gives way. He finds himself waist deep in the water, the current and cold trying to pull his feet out from beneath him. Sputtering, coughing, Dale flails out and collapses on the log. Then he sees her edging toward Patrick. "Chantel," he yells. "Chantel. Don't."

Wind barrels snow down the river. A shiver runs down Chantel's spine as the ice beneath her cracks. Standing up, she inches her way across, eyes intent on Patrick. The snow and clouds filter moonlight over him as Kenny's giggles pull him closer to the open water.

"Patrick. Patrick. Stop… Stop, please," she calls above the wind. "I can't let you do this."

He turns and stares at her.

"Patrick, when my mother died, I was lonely just like you. So I partied. Turned to boys like you have to me. Love hurts. But it also heals." She stretches her hand out to him.

He stares into the black water, takes a step forward, abruptly turns and falls against her, the river ice barely holding. His teeth chatter and he's shaking uncontrollably. She presses herself into the rise and fall of his chest.

"It's okay."

Chantel takes his hand and carefully leads him back to shore.

=

Patrick sticks to his bedroom. Skips classes and study hall. All he can do is think of her.

One day, Patrick comes home from school. Not bothering to ask why his father is home early, Patrick turns up the stairs. The door to Dale's bedroom is ajar. He's gone.

"I took him to the bus station," Henry says before Patrick has even reached the living room.

"Why?"

"'Cause he asked me. Figures we're better off without him."

"Where're the keys?"

"To what?"

"The truck."

Henry motions to a drawer, resigned. Patrick grabs them and rushes out the door.

"Just don't get pulled over."


Dale is lined up for the bus parked in front of the depot when Patrick pulls up across the street.

He sprints across. "Can you get me on as a swamper?"

"Yes. Uh, no."

"What do you mean, no?"

"Because."

"Because why?"

"Because you're still in school."

"I quit."

"Just 'cause you got caught with a teacher doesn't mean you get to quit school."

"We were studying."

"Maybe if I'd a did more studying like that, I'd a stayed in school." A voice calling out the final boarding announcement echoes off the depot's exterior walls.

"You said you could get me on."

Dale thumbs north. "Do you know what my home is? It's a room in a camp in the middle of fuck all. Two weeks in, one week out—so long as I don't get hurt or killed. When I'm done, some other loser takes my bed. My life is twelve-hour days, seven-day weeks. Then what? A month on a bender? A good time with some small-town skank? I'm not taking you down that road." He breaks out in a smile. "Come on. You've already lived every high-school boy's dream."

"It wasn't like that."

"Uhuh."

"I won't ever feel that way again. I mean, it never happens twice."

"Most of us are lucky if it happens once."

They look at each other, uncertain as to what to say next. Dale turns to the sound of the bus engine revving.

"Tell you what, finish out the school year and I'll see what I can do. A couple of summers swamping'll pay your college fees."

Dale stares at the truck. Finger-triggers Patrick.

"Don't let the cops catch you. You don't have a licence."

"At least I have insurance."

Dale breaks out in a grin. "On my dime. Don't forget it." A second rev and plume of diesel signals that the driver's patience is wearing thin.

"Gotta go."

With a wink and a nod Patrick watches as Dale disappears into the bus.

=

Years later, pursued by memory and longing, following a six-week French immersion program in Jonquière for a university credit, Patrick would spend a week in Montréal, looking for her. He stood on a tree-lined street in the shadow of Mont-Royal, across from her large home with its manicured lawn and watched through the window as Chantel cradled a baby in her arms. Her husband, a handsome man, who by now was well into his medical career, stood beside her. Like the newborn, Chantel had cradled Patrick, cared for him, possessed him as she pulled him through his darkest hour. Yet there had been a price to pay. He was still too young to put a finger on it, yet he knew that despite what she had taught him when he was fifteen, she had cheated him out of something precious.

Twenty years later, he would finally understand the damage done and how it had distorted his view of love.

# TIMBITS AND A DOUBLE-DOUBLE

Dale is waiting at the front entrance of the Peace River Regional Hospital when Patrick arrives. His jaundiced eyes light up at the sight of his brother. He smiles, revealing gums damagd by the cancer treatments. Grey skin hangs off his cheekbones.

Seeing his older brother with a cigarette between his nicotine-stained fingers and the tail of his hospital gown dangling limply around him overwhelms Patrick—as if he is somehow responsible. This Dale is a stark contrast to the man he remembers strutting around the neighbourhood flexing his pecs as he trawled through girls, leaving a trail of broken hearts in his wake.

Now Dale can barely hold his head up. He crushes his cigarette into the receptacle and anticipates Patrick's embrace with willowed arms. Patrick senses he could push his brother over with less force than a mild breeze, this the man who took pride in having laboured in the oil patch. "*One bad sniff'll kill you.*" They hug. Dale's breath smells. They turn and shuffle through the entrance doors, their pace determined by Dale's slight limp, the result of a drilling pipe he'd dropped on his foot years ago. Dale continued to work, high on painkillers, until his fourteen-day shift was over before having it looked at. "*Just like Bobby Baun,*" he used to brag, referring to the hockey hero who scored the winning goal for the Toronto Maple Leafs on a broken leg in the 1964 Stanley Cup final.

=

Dale is the last remnant of a life Patrick had long ago put behind him. Communication over the years between them, at first by phone, then by email, had dwindled to nothing. When Patrick answered Dale's call, it took him a minute to recognize the voice on the other end. The rasped sound of a smoker's voice echoed over the phone.

"Hey, little brother. It's me."

"It's been a long time."

"Sorry to bother you."

"How're you doing?"

"Uh, not so good. I thought I should phone you and uh, let you know that I've got"—Patrick listened as a stream of phlegm rose from the back of Dale's throat and reverberated through the phone—"well, I've got the big C." He took a breath. "Pancreatic."

Patrick had always assumed that Dale would die of something more aligned with his lifestyle. Cirrhosis of the liver. A car accident.

"How long?"

"Maybe a month. It's one of those fast-moving sons of bitches."

"Have you told Barbara? Susan?"

As well as having two ex-wives and an ex-significant other, Dale had five estranged adult children scattered throughout the West.

"Last I heard, Barb was in Arizona. I haven't got a clue about Susan."

"What about the kids?"

"I can't see any of 'em driving way the hell up here to take care of me. Especially Ellen. I guess you wouldn't know now, would you? She's due in November. Her guy, Carl—hell, if he didn't follow in the footsteps of Jesus Christ and become a carpenter. He's banging two-by-fours on housing projects in Calgary. First carpie I ever met who prefers wine over beer. Could I have Bordeaux with my Big Mac please and thank you."

"Ellen turned out okay."

"Damn right she did. It didn't take her long to see that living on the streets—of course it was my fault 'cause I wasn't around—is not all it's cracked out to be. I thought for sure the cops would find her in some alley with a needle stuck in her arm. She comes home, goes to college, and before you know it, she's making $75K a year pulling crap outta people's mouths." He takes a shallow breath. "I can't imagine picking food from between someone's teeth all day. Have you been flossing?" he added with a female-sounding lilt. There was a pause. "Paddy, I'm not one to ask for favours, but I sure could use a hand. You know, getting everything in order." Except for their father, who he hasn't spoken to in years, Dale didn't have anyone left to turn to.

Patrick closed his eyes.

"Should be easy for you," Dale continued, "you being a lawyer and all."

"Wills and estates aren't my area."

"That's all done. Hey, 'member that insurance guy who sold the ol' man those insurance policies after mom died? *You don't want things to go to probate, now you do?* What a piece of work he was. Either way, I made you executor. Hope you don't mind?" Patrick heard the fear and loneliness in his voice. "No one else is around."

"Then what are you going to do?"

"Haven't quite figured that part out yet."

Patrick hung up the phone and began to mentally shift his schedule before telling his wife Melissa that he was heading north to help out a brother he barely knew.

=

While Dale dresses, Patrick stands in the hallway listening to Dr. Grainger advise him that the dying often lose their appetite.

"They have more pressing matters to deal with," he says, without emotion. Knowing it would brighten Dale's spirits and allow him to be closer to family in his final days—while freeing up a hospital bed—the doctor made arrangements for a hospice bed to be available in Edmonton. "Keep him hydrated. Take a full water bottle for the drive. Make sure he drinks it."

Dale leaves the hospital without bothering to shake the doctor's hand. "He's probably pissed because I asked him if he could slip me some extra morphine so I could finish the job myself," Dale quips as he slips into the passenger seat.

They drive through Peace River's downtown to Dale's cheerless trailer. As grimy as it is gloomy, it looks and smells like it hasn't been adequately cleaned—probably not since Dale's last girlfriend. The scent of cannabis lingers in the air. Mildew dots the corners of the bathroom. The kitchen tap drips on second-hand utensils and dishes. They spend the day determining what should be sent to Dale's kids, with what's left to be picked up by the Goodwill. Patrick hires a cleaner to make the trailer look as presentable as possible before the realtor arrives.

The next day as Patrick watches the realtor put up the sign, he can't help but stare at the spot where Dale's girlfriend, Gabbie, had been found.

There had been a party. The next morning, a neighbour found her frozen body. Blood was on her nose and ears, along with a bruise down the side of her face. Dale phoned from jail.

"I'm in a bit of a pickle."

"What's happened?"

"There's not much to tell. Me an' the boys started drinking at noon. I called Gabbie and told her to come over. She had to put her kids to bed first. Then someone pulled out some coke and a bottle of tequila. By the time she arrived, we were all pretty fucked up. She joined in, then went outside for a smoke. The next thing I know the cops are shaking me awake. I think she just slipped and knocked herself out."

Dale was charged with manslaughter. Everyone at the party was too wasted to recall events with any certainty that would hold up in court. Patrick saw the charges as a way of the cops pressuring Dale into a confession. They never got one and the Crown dropped the charges.

=

The grey prairie sky fills the morning as Patrick pulls into a Tim Horton's drive-through in preparation for the drive south.

Evidence of his hospital stay wafts from Dale's pores, overriding the smell of grease, coffee, and sugar that funnels through the drive-through window. "Can you make it a double-double?" The girl's eyes widen at the sight of him. It is as if she is seeing the living dead for the first time. "And throw in a box of Timbits too, will ya?" Dale suggests, looking at Patrick for silent permission since he's the one buying. He flops back into his seat. "See. That's the difference between you and me. You're a Starbucks kinda guy, and I'm a Timmy's, camp-coffee dude."

Dale's hands tremble as he struggles to remove the lid from the cup. He leans forward and blows onto the surface, pauses, blows a second time, then a third, before pulling a Timbit from the box. Dale smiles as he playfully pokes the dough with a finger and interrogates the treat. "Do you have any final requests, the commander asks the prisoner standing in front of the firing squad?" "Can I get a Timmy's double-double and a box of Timbits?" he replies to the dough, his voice a cartoon of himself as he plops the sugary ball into his mouth. "Mmmmm, chocolate glaze," he murmurs, washing it down with a slurp of coffee. "Thank you," he adds, looking over at Patrick. Dale's rheumy eyes water slightly as he digs into a second Timbit.

Patrick eases onto the highway, a scarred spider's web of hot-oiled cracks, rolling frost heaves, and divot-sized potholes. His grip on the wheel loosens. As the car passes the town boundary, Dale salutes the welcome sign with an upturned finger.

"Good-bye, armpit of the world."

"That armpit gave you a pretty good life, I'd say."

"Fine," he growls. "Good-bye, sphincter muscle of the world. How's that?"

Dale pulls a package of smokes from his chest pocket.

"Would you grant a dying man his final wish?"

"How about a drink of water first? Doctor's orders."

He gulps down a mouthful of water, flares a match and lights up before lowering the window enough to let the smoke blow out. He purses his lips and exhales, chuckling at a weather-beaten, blue-and-white sign with an arrow pointing in the direction of a Hutterite colony.

"Did I ever tell you that I might have an extra kid? He—or she—would be an adult now, probably with kids of their own. Working the farm, I'm sure." He takes another drag. "Most city folk think young Hutterite women coming into small-town bars to expand the colony's gene pool is nothing but rural folklore. But let me tell you it ain't. The weirdest thing. No foreplay. No kissing. Just a wham-bam-thank you-madam quickie in the front seat of my pickup. 'Course I was drunk, but that's beside the point. But, you know, just as I'm putting my junk away, I look across the parking lot and see these two old guys with long beards—you know that male Hutters grow beards but not mustaches—they're just sittin' in the front of this huge dual-axle Dodge Ram truck and glaring at me. Damn if they hadn't been watching the whole time. It's like I'm some stud mounting their filly. Which I was, am, of course. The girl sees them looking at me and me looking at them. One of 'em nods and then without so much as a thank-you kiss, she hightails it out of my truck and into theirs. Now that's gratitude for you."

He flicks saliva off his lower lip with his tongue, looking at Patrick with a calm resignation, and is soon asleep, face flaccid against the passenger-door window, breath laboured, interrupted by a guttural sound that comes from deep within. Occasionally, he cracks his dry lips and mumbles something as he shifts in his seat, a Timbit curled in his fingers.

Patrick's only companion is the provincial public-radio station, its folksy announcers talking arts, hog futures, and politics. There's an election in the air. The pundits think the NDP might have a real chance at forming the next government. The drive's monotony, bordered by northern forest and intermittently by scraggy farmland, is broken up by long-haul trucks that swoosh by, hip-checking the car with bursts of passing air. He glances at his brother. No matter how much Patrick tries to distance himself, he has never been able to escape the fact that he is still part of a long-established story with an arc and terminus soon to be reached. It's not that he is embarrassed or indifferent to Dale's story or the choices he made. No matter how Patrick looks at it, he feels a sense of guilt that, unlike him, Dale never found a way to fly.

When his left knee begins to go numb from the drive, Patrick pulls into a truck stop and gently shakes Dale awake.

"Hungry?" he asks.

Dale shakes his head.

"Nothing like a greasy burger and fries mixed with a bit of chemo to make your day."

"Funny," Dale replies. "But first," he says, pulling on the passenger-door handle as he slides out of the seat and makes a beeline to the men's room.

Dewlaps of fat roll off the young waitress's chin. There's a small-town tawdriness about her. As she scribbles down the order, the waitress avoids Dale's gaze. The brothers wait for their food, looking around at everything but each other.

Three booths down, an old couple huddle over their plates. The woman's long hair is thin, more grey than gold. The purple sweater she's wearing with jeans and pink slippers is frayed at the cuffs. Patrick stares at her companion. A ragged baseball cap barely contains stringy grey hair streaming over his ears. The man's face is a rugged map of a life spent outdoors. Large, jaundiced eyes bulge out. Light through oversized glasses accentuate paw-sized smudges on the lens. A bolo tie with a turquoise and silver pendant cinches a black-and-blue plaid shirt with pearl snaps. His jeans are as filthy as they are tattered. The cowboy boot sticking into the aisle has a wide split at the toe. He sits hunched over his plate, forearms pressed to the edge of the table, both hands firmly on his hamburger. It is clear by the way his mouth sinks into the jaw that he does not possess any teeth. He nibbles at his meal. The couple do not exchange a single word.

Dale follows Patrick's gaze. "Guy looks like our old man on a good day," he whispers. "Speaking of which, how is the ol' geezer?"

"He's on a secure floor now."

"I guess that's Alzheimer's for stage-four cancer?"

"If you say so."

"At least I can say I beat him to something."

"If you say so," Patrick repeats, his voice dry, knowing you shouldn't win an argument with a dying man. "Do you want to see him? Maybe say goodbye?

"There's no point, is there? I doubt if he'd even know who I was."

"That's not the point."

"What *is* the point then?"

The woman wipes gravy from the plate with a piece of white bread. She stares past them as she plops the bread into her mouth.

"Think she'd look like that?"

"Who?"

"Our mother."

"What makes you think that?"

"Don't all old people kinda look the same?"

"I never thought of it like that."

"Can we see her? You know, one last time."

"Sure." Patrick knows that the living must respect the wishes of the dying.

"*Mucho-gracias.*" Dale chuckles. "That's the limit of my Spanish. That and, '*Me gustaría una cerveza.*'" He helps himself to one of Patrick's fries. "It sure is strange," he says, popping the strip of fried potato into his mouth.

"What?"

"Dying."

Dale's features, cut deep from hard living and disease, make his words sound worse than they are, like the time he joked to Patrick that he hadn't tried heroin because he was scared of needles.

"This isn't our first grim-reaper rodeo together, now is it?"

"You're right there, pardner."

"You're one up on me, aren't you, in that department?"

Dale's eyes narrow. "Can't you let a man die in peace?"

"That was a cheap shot. Sorry."

"What's done is done."

The man slides out of his seat. He stands, spreads his feet and waits. Patrick watches. Offers up a polite smile as the woman grips the edge of the Formica table with one hand. She places the other on the top of the red vinyl booth and slides her way out, one small step at a time. Once in the aisle, she pauses to steady herself, head and shoulders stooped awkwardly forward. The muscles twitch in the man's arms and shoulders as he takes her by the elbow. He stares at Patrick and Dale, as if to say "*What are you looking at?*" She mumbles something incoherent. "It's okay, honey. We'll be home soon," he says, his voice low. He holds her firmly, tenderly, gentlemanly. They shuffle past Dale and Patrick, towards the door.

=

As they near the city, muted particles of yellow-orange light filter through grey cloud. Crossing the North Saskatchewan River on the High-Level bridge, Dale looks downstream trying to catch a glimpse of the spot around the bend where their brother Kenny had drowned so many years ago.

"You ever go back there?" Dale asks.

"It's been a while."

They stop at the convenience store kitty-corner from the municipal cemetery. Dale picks out the most expensive bouquet he can find and hands it to Patrick.

It takes them a few minutes to remember where she is buried. Patrick follows and watches as Dale brushes off a layer of summer dust from the flat, grey, granite gravestone before placing the flowers at its base.

"I'd be a different kinda person if she hadn'ta died," Dale says, his eyes fixed on the ground.

"We'd both be."

"At least they got him."

"They did indeed."

He turns to Patrick. "I guess I'll be seeing her pretty soon." He gazes up into the sky. "Hmmm, maybe not, given my record," he continues in a whisper. He pulls a brown envelope from his jacket and holds it out to Patrick.

"I fucked up pretty good."

"We all fuck up at one time or another."

"Some more than others." Tears well in the corners of Dale's eyes. He stares at the stone. "I'm sorry."

"It's okay."

"No… you don't understand. I'm sorry that I hit her."

"Who?"

"Gabbie. I smacked her. I didn't mean to. She was pissed because of the mess everyone was making. You know what parties are like. She was mad, knowing she'd be the one left to clean up in the morning. I'd have helped her. But you know me. I was higher than a kite." Dale is sobbing now, saying things Patrick can barely make out. He wipes his palm across his mouth, his voice shaking. "I was high. I was angry. At her. At my exes. At my kids. I didn't hit her hard. At least that's what I thought. She went outside and passed out. Froze. It was an accident. Do you understand? An accident."

Patrick pulls Dale into him. "She died of exposure. That was the coroner's conclusion." As the warmth of Dale's tears fall onto his face, a breeze brings the flowers to life.

"I guess when you're dying you realize that being angry your whole life doesn't do you a hill a beans," Dale laughs, tears still running down his cheeks. "My Confucius moment."

The sun is disappearing behind the cemetery trees as they walk back to the car. Patrick's hand rests brotherly across Dale's back.

Two weeks later, Dale is gone. Patrick hangs up the phone after taking the call from the hospice, overwhelmed less by grief or sorrow than by a quiet sadness. That night, as he sits on his deck, a glass of wine in hand, he opens the envelope. Inside, along with the will, are printouts of Internet searches about Gabbie's girls, Susan and Angela. Following Gabbie's death, her parents had taken them back to Saskatchewan. Judging by the pictures that Dale had of the girls, Patrick guesses that Gabbie had been a good-looking woman. Susan, the elder of the two, is about to graduate from high school. Angela is two years behind her. Dale has left everything to them. The proceeds from the sale of the trailer and a small life-insurance policy won't be much, but maybe enough to give them the leg up Dale had never had.

# APART TOGETHER

Patrick is up early for a Saturday morning. The night before he'd told his wife that he would be going into the office to prepare for an upcoming labour tribunal hearing. The owners of a pulp and paper mill in the Peace Country—American, of course— were attempting to use an obscure angle to do a run-around with their obligations to the workers' pension plan. They can try to screw workers all they want— as long as it is legal. Patrick is a partner in a boutique firm specializing in labour law. He's been practising for almost twenty years. He still remembers tacking a sign behind his desk that still hangs there today— *It is easier to fuck someone around than it is to give a fuck.*

Before going into the office, Patrick would grant his brother his final wish. His plan included a small liberty, one that at least in Patrick's mind, would, if Dale were alive, bring him some solace and sense of closure. Patrick had packed the urn, along with a trowel and gardening gloves, in the trunk of the car the night before. He filled his coffee mug, grabbed a bottle of water from the kitchen and trod softly across the tiled floor. As Patrick made his way to the front door, he paused to gaze up the stairs, knowing he would rather still be in bed with Melissa.

Outside, a familiar sense of early May's last gasp of winter greeted him. Even with the sun arching over the eastern horizon, a cool wind pressed into Patrick. He sat in the front seat of his car, waiting for the rushing air from the vents to heat up, the metal coffee mug, embossed in black lettering—*Fitzpatrick and Company Lawyers*—his only source of warmth. He took small sips. Mentally mapped out his day. He had to be home before the trash haulers arrived. He put the car into drive and headed towards the cemetery.

Traffic was light, devoid of the congestion and noise of weekday commuters. The streets and boulevards remained chalked in dust and gravel laid down over the winter months. Patrick often drove to work without the distraction of morning radio chatter. It gave him time to think as well as a sense of calm and quietness to his morning. Today, however, he turned the radio to the same public radio station he and his brother had listened to a month ago when Patrick had volunteered to bring Dale from his home in the northern part of the province to the hospice in the city.

It was just past seven when Patrick arrived at the cemetery. It was quiet, except for the hum of distant traffic and the occasional caw of magpies frolicking in the trees. He knew that the city workers, if they had a scheduled Saturday burial, wouldn't arrive until eight. Patrick parked the car as close to his mother's grave as he could. Long after her death, grief and sorrow had weighed him down, pressing down on him, until finally the day came when he realized nothing except memories was all that was left. It had taken a few false starts before he married and formed a family of his own; Melissa and Jena, the product of Melissa's high school sweetheart who left her the day Melissa announced she was pregnant. Jena was living in Montreal, completing her M.A. at McGill. Then there was the free-spirited Lynn, the product of Melissa and Patrick's union. She was taking a gap year from the rigours of engineering, living in Tofino, waitressing and learning to surf cold water.

The sun now filled in the sky. It was bright yellow against the blue prairie sky, the same as it had been the day Patrick's mother had been murdered years ago. He thought of her last words to him as she stepped out the door that day, words that any fourteen-year-old would dismiss. "*Be careful. I love you.*"

Never doubting the illegality of his plan, Patrick was determined to grant Dale's request to inter his ashes with their mother, certain there must be a provincial statute, a municipal by-law, if nothing else the common courtesy of asking permission before proceeding, that he simply ignored. What was the worst that could happen?

As Patrick slipped on the gardening gloves, he sized up the adjoining plot. It was reserved for his father. With Henry now deep into the depths of Alzheimer's, Patrick knew it wouldn't be long before a return trip to the cemetery would be required. He also knew that when his long-estranged father passed away, he and Melissa would probably be only ones in attendance at his service. He opened the car door, tucked the trowel into his left back pocket, jammed the bottle of water into the right front pocket of his jacket, cupped the bottom urn with his hands, and tramped toward the grave.

Patrick stood in front of the grey granite gravestone. Inhaled, then exhaled, with a respectful breath. Sensed a twinge building in his abdomen. Even after all these years, visiting his mother brought out an unutterable sadness, a sense of longing for what might have been. He grinned. "Hey. How are you?"

A grunt accompanied his knees hitting the ground. The cold from the soil seeped through his jeans. He surveyed a place near the head of the grave, eyeballed the urn, and began to cut a circle in the grass, digging just deep enough to reach the roots. The smell of earth, pungent, pleasant, reminded Patrick of the upcoming May long weekend when he and Melissa—assuming there would be no final blast of winter—would spend time in the yard, planting, cleaning up, preparing for the short growing season. Patrick grasped the grass with his fingers and pulled. Roots tore from the soil, reminding him of crumbling rock.

He set the scalp of grass aside and continued with the digging. The spring sun had softened the top layer of soil, initially making his task easy. The deeper he dug, the harder it got. Patrick soon hit semi-frozen soil. Ice glued the dirt together. He used the trowel to chip away at the dirt, leveraging it against the ground to pop out bits and chunks, spraying bits of soil into the air, his face, his eyes. A hint of ammonia flared his nostrils. The effort required to dig such a small hole was a reminder of the weight Patrick had gained over the years. Even with his jacket now off and only a ratty hoodie to protect him from the spring breeze, the rising heat from his body ringed his collar. Sweat built on his back. He resisted the temptation to take the hoodie off, knowing he would only get colder. He paused to catch his breath and stare into the small hole, then gripped the trowel handle with both hands, sucked in his breath, and attacked it.

Hole now dug, Patrick slipped off the gloves, and caught his breath while admiring his work. The morning breeze carried sweat from his brow. Patrick gently rubbed his thumb over his wedding ring, a reminder that Melissa would now be awake, more than likely reading the morning paper over a cup of coffee with the cat for company. He reached over and grabbed the water bottle. As he sipped, Patrick stared at the flat headstone. It was a simple stone, the only inscription: Maureen Elizabeth Fitzpatrick. Date of her birth. The date of her death.

As he reached over to grab the urn, the muscles around his ribs and shoulders resisted the effort. He held the urn over the hole in front of him. He pressed the urn into place, ensuring it was deep enough and reasonably level. With his brother's ashes now in their final resting place, Patrick leaned forward and scooped the small mound of dirt with his hands and forearms into the hole, partially filling it. He pressed it down with his hands before returning for more, which he pressed down as well. He then returned the mat of grass. Trying to make the area look as undisturbed as possible, Patrick filled the remaining gaps in the ground. Task completed, he stood, tamped down the area with his foot and emptied the remaining water over the grass. Gazing around to ensure there was no one around, he cupped the remaining soil into his hands, took a few steps and scattered it as far as he could. He gave the site a final finish, sweeping and rubbing the area clean. He then stood and bowed his head respectfully. "I hope you two meet again."

As he walked back to the car, Patrick patted the outside pocket of his jacket, double-checking to ensure that the small plastic bag containing the ashes he had removed from Dale's urn were still there.

=

Joggers, dog walkers and families passed Patrick as he stood on the edge of the path that ran parallel to the river. Spring runoff was not yet complete. The water surged past. Jagged saws of ice—dangerous, deadly in its weakened state—protruded from the banks. The fort where the brothers—Dale, Patrick, and Kenny—had played as children, was long gone, replaced with mountain ash, dogwood and sweetgrass. Tracks of small animals—mice and rabbits—plotted across patches of remaining snow shaded from the sun by bushes and trees. Shadows congealed the river.

A cold turbulence rose in Patrick's chest as he stared at the tree where Kenny had fallen off and through the ice when he was twelve. The branch on which he had crawled out onto the river had long ago been amputated, a stub the only evidence that it had ever existed. Patrick followed the lines of the tree. My, how you've grown, he thought. If you could talk, what would you say? What would reach deep into the cosmos and reassure Dale that it wasn't his fault? Patrick looked to the right of the tree at a small depression in the bank. Two years after Kenny's death, Patrick, Dale, and Henry watched as Maureen slipped into the river at that very spot. She stood in the rushing water, tears streaming down her cheeks, asking God to let her see her baby one more time. Her request denied, Maureen upended the urn and dumped her son's ashes into the water before throwing the brushed green aluminum container as far out into the river as she could.

Clutching the plastic bag in his hand, Patrick squatted over a small eddy on the edge of the river. He unzipped the bag. Stared at the pulverized grey, brown fragments of teeth and bone. This is it, he said to himself. When I'm gone that'll be the end of the line. It was with the birth of Lynne that he realized the finality of it all, knowing that with his death, the Fitzpatrick chain would be broken, once and for all.

He turned the open bag over, hoping, as Dale's remains trickled through the water, forming a small anthill on top of the black-brown mud on the bottom, that this final gesture might somehow give his brother the closure he had sought his whole life, that big brother and little brother would be reunited in spirit if nothing else.

As he neared the parking lot, Patrick stopped at an opening in the trees and gazed out across the river. Inexplicably, the lyrics of a Talking Heads song sprang up in his mind … *in a beautiful house, with a beautiful wife. And you may ask yourself, well, how did I get here?*

And he wondered, how did I get where I don't belong? He turned and headed home.

=

Patrick sits at the kitchen counter, the remnants of his lunch beside him on a small plate. The labour file folder is beside the plate, unopened. Melissa's response to becoming an empty-nester and, Patrick dare not say, the onset of menopause, was to go on a house-cleaning tear. Hence the call to the trash haulers. There's leftover stuff from old weekend jobs— bits of wood, drywall—that's done nothing but collect dust over the years. An old lawnmower that never did work properly after Patrick's miserable repair attempt sits in the corner of the garage covered in a tarp, giving off gas fumes. The extra room in the basement is now a storage room/ museum of gifts from Christmases gone by—toys and mementos that Melissa thought she would save in the eventuality of becoming a grandmother. The rest was junk, pure junk, stuff that couldn't, in good conscience, be given away to a charity.

"You okay?" Melissa asks, concern on her face as she steps into the kitchen, a yoga mat stuck under her arm. She affectionately runs her hand over his shoulders. Her eyes swelled with tears when Patrick told her how he had spent his morning. "Such a good man," she said with a kiss. "Brother. Father."

They met on a city bus. Like many young transit drivers, Patrick bid on routes that stopped at the university or one of the colleges. It was a great way to idly pass the time gazing over the cover of a good paperback as eye candy got on and off the bus. Reading on layovers, partially to counter the boredom that comes with driving a forty-foot taxi all day, also came with a secondary objective of impressing passengers. Patrick had the added benefit of actually being a student. He was taking an online university course: *An Anthology of Canadian English.* Having strategically tucked the book into the netted pouch on the side of the driver's seat—front cover facing out—it was nearly impossible for a boarding passenger to miss. When Melissa stepped onto the bus, she paid no mind to the book or Dale's cheerful greeting. Without a word, she strode to the back of the bus, picked an empty seat with the clear intent of wanting to be left alone. Patrick looked at her through the rear-view mirror. Despite her being cloaked in winter clothes, Patrick could see that she was a beauty. Older than the average straight-out-of-high-school college student, it was clear the woman was the serious type.

She spent her time on the bus with her nose in a book. Aside from an occasional look in the rear-view mirror, Patrick tried not to pay her any attention—until later that night when she stepped back onto the bus, this time clutching her own edition of *An Anthology of Canadian English*. The bus was pretty much empty. As Melissa climbed the steps, she glanced at his dog-eared version as she settled into the nearest available seat. "Have you read any of Alice Munro's stories?"

"Not yet. I'm taking my courses through correspondence. I get a bit of leeway on what and when I read."

"Nice."

"And you?"

"I'm plodding through. I'm also trying to get through *The Collected Works of Billy the Kid* in my spare time."

"*The Collected Works of Billy the Kid?*"

"Michael Ondaatje?"

Blood rushed to Patrick's cheeks.

"You'll have to read it sometime."

"What are you going to do with an English degree?" Patrick asked, assuming this was her major.

"I'm going to be a teacher."

"Elementary...my dear Watson."

She rolled her eyes. It was not one of Patrick's better opening lines. Then she smiled.

"A bus driver who studies Canadian literature? Very Jack Kerouac-ish," Melissa said with a wink as she stepped off the bus, leaving through the front door rather than the back.

"*On the Road*," Patrick replied, with a smile.

That this woman with deep blue eyes, strong cheeks, and a sweet, subtle smile, was studying to be a unionized teacher made Patrick think of his mother. Soon after Dale dropped out of high school he started dating a hairdresser called Belinda, or as Maureen referred to her, the ditz. Over supper one night, his mother told Dale in no uncertain terms that he should dump her. *Find yourself a nurse or a teacher, a woman with a strong union behind her,* she said, knowing, as only a mother can, that it would take a no-nonsense woman with a stable job to settle Dale down and keep him grounded.

Six months later Patrick and Melissa moved in together. It was as natural if they had been meant for each from the day they met. Melissa soon graduated and began teaching. In order to make ends meet while completing his studies, Patrick continued to drive a bus on the weekends. Coming from a union environment, he was drawn towards left-leaning writers—Orwell, Sinclair, Engels. It was his thesis advisor, Professor Blecha, who pointed Patrick in the direction of law school when Patrick told him he was thinking of pursuing a PhD.

"PhDs are a dime a dozen," Blecha said. "Have you ever thought of law?"

"Lawyers are a dime a dozen too. And, I'd have to wear a tie."

"But you are going to be a more effective advocate for social change through the courts rather than through books," Blecha continued. "Wearing a tie," he continued, "is a small price to pay for justice."

To this day, Patrick remembers Melissa's response when he told her he was going to write the law school admissions test. *You can be anything you want to be. You just need to put your mind to it.* That was all he needed.

Patrick swivels on the stool and watches Melissa as she walks to the front door. Sunlight filters down from the grey mottled afternoon sky. Sparkles through tendrils of her hair.

She turns and smiles. "Love you."

It is moments like this that Patrick wonders how it is possible to love someone as much as he loves her.

"And make sure they take the branches from around the back of the garage," she reminds him with a wink, knowing that there is a good chance he will forget.

They live in a large house on the southwest side of the North Saskatchewan River, on a  curved street with a two-car garage and a lawn and garden that are impeccably manicured during the summer. It is a world away from the strip malls, trucker hotels and drab stucco detached houses, bordered by chain-link fences and scrubby lawns, where Patrick grew up.

The irony is not lost on Patrick that some of the people in the neighbourhood where he now lives—the businessmen, the lawyers, the upper-middle-class echelons of society—are grown-up versions of kids he used to loathe. When he was in high school, the chance to play against the newer larger schools with their uppity students—whether it be football, basketball or track—was an incentive in and of itself. What the east end boys lacked in spit and polish they made up for with a collective determination. At times, their unsettling anger and desire to kick the shit out of each and every one of those spoiled south side pricks was the chance for them to show what they were made of. A well-aimed hit after the whistle? A shot to the ribs with an elbow? Merely getting even.

There are days while waiting in the hallway outside the courtroom, Patrick will sometimes recognize the faces of former high school foes. The interaction varies, from a warm handshake and the exchange of business cards to a distant, professional, nod. The parallels between football and a courtroom have never been lost on Patrick. A judge, sombre, serious, is now the referee with words and logic replacing elbows and grit.

=

Patrick hears the truck before he sees it. He rises and stares out from the living room window as a three-ton truck, white with green lettering You Holler—We'll Hauler pulls to the curb. The truck is caked in a slew of mud and road salt. Brown sludge clings to the wheel guards. The cargo bed bursts with rusting appliances, rotting wood, old bikes, and all sorts of consumer throw-aways. Two clean-cut college-aged kids, crisp in green overalls, mud from the ankles down, jump out of the truck and saunter to the door. Patrick greets them with a quick reminder about the branches. Better for it to be on their plate than his. The two are well versed in the pleasantries necessary for a decent tip—all the while giving a modicum of professionalism to a job nobody else wants to do. He wishes them well and tells them that if the need arises, they are welcome to use the washroom by going through the garage.

As he settles into giving the labour hearing material the attention it requires, the doorbell rings. He sighs and strides to the door, prepared to remind whoever it is at the door where the bathroom is.

It is immediately clear that the man in front of Patrick is someone who has spent his life working outside. Thick-shouldered, legs spread apart, he stands on the front stoop. He is around Patrick's age. Like Patrick, he has put on middle-age weight but has managed to retain a boyish handsomeness; grey hair buzzed almost to the point of being bald, eyes salt-water grey-blue, and a sharp jaw from which a small flap of skin hangs. His coveralls are crisp and clean. Parked at the curb is a fully decked-out Ford F-350. Its paint job matches the five-ton. Patrick's eyes narrow as he sees the name on the bottom of the truck door—Lance Mueller. Seeing his reaction, the man turns his head slightly in Patrick's direction, allowing the sun to caress his weathered skin.

"Patrick. How are you?"

"Lance?"

As Lance extends a hand, he smiles with the enthusiasm of hitting on a woman in a bar. His hands are thick, nails lined in a layer of black grime along with the crevices of his fingers, are cut short.

"It's been a while."

"Forty years or so."

The last image Patrick remembered of Lance sharpened into focus. "The last time I saw you…"

"I was being hauled off in the back of a police car." Lance shrugs his shoulder. "Shit happens."

Lance and Patrick had been friends in elementary school. It was a chaotic, impulsive, wild and at times dangerous friendship. They played road hockey together, hung out in the river valley, felt up the same girls, and shared stolen beer. Unlike Patrick, Lance was a troubled, out-of-control kid, who came from an unstable home lacking any adult guidance. There were days in the middle of a cold snap when Lance would walk to school with just a pair of cotton tube socks inside worn runners on his feet and no more than a dirty, oversized hand-me-down jacket two sizes too big for cover. His lunch usually consisted of peanut butter and jam or a macaroni bologna sandwich with an orange thrown in. More than anything, Lance was tough. He would take a shit-kicking, get back up, and take another shit-kicking until his opponent got tired of kicking the shit out of him. At school, he once challenged Steve Crowley to a fight when Steve tried to steal Lance's Oreo cookie. Steven Crowley was two years older and forty pounds heavier. But for Lance, an Oreo cookie wasn't just a cookie. It was a special treat because the only time he got an Oreo cookie was when the welfare cheque arrived at the beginning of each month.

Lance watches as his crew chucks the remaining waste into the back of the truck. "I could say that this is a mere coincidence—a customer courtesy call—but if truth be known, when I saw your name on the schedule, I thought there are only so many Patrick Fitzpatricks around."

"This is your…" Patrick says, motioning to the truck on the curb.

"The whole kit and caboodle. Ten trucks and growing."

"Impressive."

"We travelled different roads, mind you, but eventually got to the same place, wouldn't you say?"

"Your road was a helluva lot tougher than mine ever was."

"I dunno. Having your mom die like that. I heard they got the guy."

"It took some time. But yes."

"You know I went to juvie for a while. Right?"

"That's what I heard."

"Six months. Then three years of foster care."

"Sorry to hear."

"I always liked your mom though. She always had a smile on her face. Even when she was giving us shit. I wish I could say the same about mine. But, hey," Lance says with a shrug. "What's the saying, you can pick your nose but you can't pick your parents."

Patrick had always felt a bit sorry for Lance. His mother was one of the prettiest women in the neighbourhood. She was tall and slender with long black Rapunzel hair that cascaded down to her waist. She always greeted Patrick with a smile. Yet, as Maureen often noted, there were always men around her, helping her out with yard work, taking her to the store, on dates. Lance used to brag about his adventures with his mother's various boyfriends, like the time one left them penniless at Sylvan Lake. He told them he was going for ice cream and never came back. Social services provided them with bus fare home. Things turned for the worse when Lance's mother started dating a jail guard.

The crew finishes securing the load. "Hey," Lance hollers. "Double check everything. Make sure it's secure. If you get a ticket for an unsafe load it comes out of your pay." He turns to Patrick. "How'd they do?"

"Quick. Efficient. Polite."

"Hope you didn't tip em."

Before Patrick can respond, Lance turns his head and releases the crew with a dismissive nod. "See you back at the shop." He holds up a hand as Patrick reaches for his wallet. "This ain't a restaurant."

They watch the truck pull away.

"Nice kids. But they never last. They find the work too hard. Too dirty. Hours too long. Kids today. They're as disposable as the stuff we haul away."

Disposable.

It reminded Patrick of the time Lance, fighting back the tears, told him how his mom had thrown one of his sister's used tampons at him and told him he was as useless and as disposable. It was soon after the tampon episode that Patrick saw the man Lance would almost kill. He was a stocky, powerful-looking man with greasy hair and a menacing stare meant to intimidate. He was a guard at the remand centre and from what Patrick heard later, thought that prison thuggery could also be used just as effectively on the home front. It wasn't long before Lance started to come to school with bruises. One night the boyfriend decided to lay one beating too many on Lance's mother. Patrick watched from his bedroom window as the police and ambulance came to a roaring stop in front of the house. Soon after, paramedics pulled the gurney from inside the house and hauled the man away. Lance and his mom, draped in blankets, soon followed. A cigarette glowed in her fingers. She held a dishtowel to her cheek. They were led to separate cruisers. Soon after, social workers arrived to take Lance's sister and younger brothers away. When the police interviewed Maureen, Patrick listened from the stairs. The police told Maureen that the two had been drinking. One thing led to the other and they were soon yelling and screaming at each other. The man was on top of his mother, beating her, when Lance charged into the living room, baseball bat in hand. Before the man could say a word, Lance cracked him in the ribs with the bat. The man rolled over onto his back, fully exposed. Lance then teed up the guy's balls with the bat and let him have it. In a matter-of-fact tone, the female cop informed Maureen that the guy would be lucky to pee again, never mind get an erection. Serves him right, Maureen said with a nod.

Coffee in hand, the two men sit on the front stoop staring as the crisp spring breeze blows winter dust into the air.

"You're a lawyer, right?" Lance said. "I've read about you in the paper."

Over the years, newspapers had given Patrick a glimpse into Lance's life too. His brother Tony had been sentenced to ten years in prison for manslaughter after stabbing a man to death during a party. Several years ago, a woman with the same name as Lance's mother died in a car crash outside of the city. It was then that Patrick wondered if Lance was still alive.

Lance begins to pull a cigarette package out of his pocket. Noting Patrick's gaze, he puts it away. "Not exactly politically correct now, is it?"

"How'd you get into this?" Patrick asks, motioning to the trucks.

"I was gonna ask you the same thing. How'd you get into lawyering?" Lance paused. "You always were smarter than the average bear." He chuckles as he takes a sip from his cup. "You were breaking the law long before you were upholding it. Remember the time we shoplifted?"

"Grade eight."

"Code eleven."

The two men break out in laughter.

"Wow. You remember code eleven," Lance says, a sparkle in his eyes.

"How could I forget?"

Before shipping him off to juvenile detention for beating up a teacher, Tony showed his younger brother Lance the tricks of the shoplifting trade. It was particularly easy at Zeller's because, according to Tony, they had fewer security people roaming the store. Tony emphasized that the key to shoplifting was to have a reliable partner and to always be aware of what was being said over the public address system. "Code" meant shoplifter. The number referred to the section of the store where the shoplifters were.

"I only did it to impress Sally Washington," Lance says with a chuckle.

"If I recall, she was a pretty busy girl."

"That she was."

Sally was thirteen but was already hanging around with the older high school boys. Lance figured that by proffering Sally the jewellery she wanted, he could convince her to go a matinee movie with him, maybe let him feel her up. Enticed by adventure, a share in the proceeds, and Lance's potential dream date, Patrick agreed to become his partner-in-crime.

"We each take off to separate exits," Lance told Patrick as they stepped into the store, knowing that the in-store wannabe cop could only collar them one at a time. The intentions of these two hanging around the jewellery section of a department store were clear. Lance and Patrick might as well have hung shoplifter signs over their necks. Patrick shook in his boots trying to be as cool as a twelve-year-old could be while Lance nonchalantly eyed the goods, trying to act as though he was truly interested in buying something. The woman behind the counter eyed them. As she turned her attention to a customer, Patrick watched wide-eyed as Lance curled a gold necklace into his hand and slipped it into his pocket. Just as quickly, he took a silver ring and did the same thing. They headed to the exit.

"Code eleven. Code eleven," echoed over the air.

"Shit," Lance hissed, picking up the pace.

Patrick looked around, half expecting a squad of policemen in SWAT gear to come storming around the corner. Instead, a huge man, with jowls that flapped like a bowl of Jell-O, appeared at the end of the aisle. He growled, "Hold it right there."

"Run," Lance yelled, flinging the necklace into the security guard's face.

Unfortunately for him, the security goombah didn't know who he was dealing with when he grabbed Lance by the scruff of the neck and spun him around. Lance clamped onto the guard's hand with his teeth and bit down hard, drawing blood. The guy screamed. As he clutched his hand, Lance kicked him square in the kneecap. The guy howled and fell to the floor. Lance and Patrick burst through the front door and hightailed it across the parking lot, half expecting a squad of police cars to come barrelling down the street. The crisp spring air—still tinged with winter—filled their lungs as they sprinted, panting, sweating— laughing profusely, to the sanctity of the river valley. Snow filled their boots. The underbrush snapped beneath their feet. They were safe knowing that the cops wouldn't bother to chase two wannabe juvenile shoplifters through the mud and the trees and the snow-covered grass. They waited it out in the fort, shivering with the cold, until the coast was clear.

Patrick studies Lance, trying to detect any remnants of the look in Lance's eyes that he saw that day—the manic ferocity, the viciousness on the verge of animal anger that Patrick had never seen before in his life and only saw again during his brief stint as a Crown prosecutor. He raises an eyebrow as his eyes wander past Lance and reads the block writing on the panel of the truck bed for the second time—Supporters of the Women's Inner-City Shelter.

Lance shrugs his shoulders. "I did it after my mother died. Besides," Lance continued, "My accountant said I needed the tax deduction."

Patrick had read about Lance's mother's death. Ten years ago, she was a passenger in a car that went off the highway north of the city. The autopsy reported that the driver's alcohol level was twice the legal limit.

"Your mother would be proud."

"It's the least I could do."

Lance crosses his arms over his chest, stares  at his truck. "You know what I like about business?"

"I assume it's the money."

"Sure, but it's much more than that. What I learned the most was that women smell money. Having something, the ability, to have something others want. I knew then and there that I would never be any good working for someone else. When I aged out of foster homes, my first job was swamping. Here I was out in the middle of nowhere, freezing my ass off, swamping drilling pipe and lubricants for some asshole redneck who didn't give a shit whether I lived or died. But I knew the day would come when I would be taking orders from nobody but…" He smiles as he presses a nail-bitten thumb into his chest. "Me. So when oil prices tanked, I started working for a guy hauling junk. It's a pretty simple business. All you need is a truck and a phone. Of course, the Internet has changed everything. But I knew I needed an edge. Something different. Rebranding is what they call it. All the other junk collectors thought I was wasting my money prettying up a truck, buying matching overalls. Now they're all trying the same thing. And you?"

"I sort of came into law in a roundabout way. I started out as a transit driver."

"Good union gig. Bus driving. I'm not a union guy. Can't afford it." He looks at Patrick as if expecting  to be reprimanded. "Hey, you an Oilers fan?"

Patrick stopped following hockey years ago. "I catch a game, here and there."

"I've got a quarter share in two seats ten rows up. So long as it's not the Flames. Or the Leafs."

"I might take you up on that," Patrick responds, politely.

With nothing else to share, the two men stand. Lance sees Patrick glance at his unadorned wedding finger and shakes his head.

"I will admit, I've never been able to figure that one out. Marriage, I mean. My first wife, she got all religious on me. Don't get me wrong. Religion's got its place. Just not in mine," he says with a sad chuckle. "I guess things just never worked out. So now I got my dogs. I got my acreage. I guess," he continues, a sly grin filling his cheeks as he spreads a hand in the direction of his truck, "I'm more or less married to the business. But you, you sound like you've done okay on the matrimonial side."

Maybe it was the lilt in Patrick's voice. Maybe it was the way he smiled when he told Lance about Melissa. Either way, as Patrick told Lance about the life the two of them had built together, a spark lit up in his eyes. A small lump swelled in his throat.

"Some guys have all the luck," Lance says, taking a step off the stoop. "Take care. And take care of that wife of yours."

"Hey Lance, you never mentioned children. Anything on that front? Just curious. You know, someone to take over the business."

An awkward pause follows. Lance stares at his boots. When he looks back up, he gazes past Patrick into the living room. Runs his hands over his face, as if trying to collect his thoughts. "I got a son. Jamie. He's got a bit of a wild streak, especially when he's been drinking. Just like his father." Lance smirks, a combination of pride and embarrassment. "I hope, I really do, that when he gets out this time, he'll have learned his lesson. I don't know. I just don't know."

"I'm sorry to hear."

"It is what it is."

Lance pulls out a baseball cap from inside his vest. The colours match the truck. There is a *You Holler We'll Hauler* patch on the front. A smile the size of an oil slick spreads across his face. He clicks his jaw. "For special clients."

Patrick pulls the cap over his head.

"Looks good on ya."

"Good seeing you, Lance. Glad to hear things worked out."

"You too." Lance bids him good-bye with a salute.

Patrick  watches as Lance ambles towards his F-350 with a cowboy bow-legged gait and climbs into the truck. The boy once destined for jail or a life of unskilled, low-paying, soul-crushing McWalmart jobs now drives a pickup truck that costs more than the down payment on a small house.

Patrick closes the door. He looks around. There are legal briefs to review. A wife to love. Grandchildren to look forward to.

## MICHAEL MAITLAND

Born in Toronto and raised in the Oshawa area, Michael moved to Edmonton during the oil boom years, where he received a BA from the University of Alberta, and then spent a year and a half travelling before moving to the north to produce videos for the NWT government. After completing an MFA in screenwriting, he moved to Victoria, where he still lives. He worked in feature films and television before turning to documentaries; feature-length documentaries he co-produced, directed and wrote include: *George Ryga: The Political Playwright, Judith Thomson: My Pyramids, Panych Plays* and *Richard Margison: The Folk Singing Opera Star* (with Bruce Cockburn). Several of his short stories have appeared in Canadian literary journals. *The World Is But a Broken Heart* is Michael's first book.

Eco-Audit
Printing this book using Rolland Enviro100 Book
instead of virgin fibres paper saved the following resources:

| Trees | Water | Air Emissions |
|-------|-------|---------------|
| 1 | 1,000 L | 208 kg |